Inspired by a true story

Other Books by Robert M. Drake

Spaceship (2012)

Science (2013)

Beautiful Chaos (2014)

Black Butterfly (2015)

A Brilliant Madness (2015)

Beautiful and Damned (2016)

Broken Flowers (2016)

For Excerpts and Updates please follow:

Instagram.com/rmdrk
Facebook.com/rmdrk
Twitter.com/rmdrk

ISBN: 978-0-9986293-0-8

Book Cover: Robert M. Drake

Cover Image licensed by Shutter Stock Inc.

ATTENTION: SCHOOLS AND BUSINESSES

Robert M. Drake books are available at quantity discounts with bulk purchase for educational, business, or sales promotional use. For information, please e-mail:
rmdrkone@gmail.com

Dedicated to Seyvn

All of my words
will always be yours.

And when it was over,
nothing defined us
other than the moments
that made us feel free.

Gravity

Robert M. Drake

1

I don't know how to start this and I don't know how it began, but I did remember a lot of things. Like the first time I rode a bike, the first time I swam in the ocean, and the first time I looked into his eyes. I remembered a lot of things. Like the way I used to laugh when I was a little girl, the light in my father's eyes when he would lift me into the air, and the way those lazy summer days would slowly pass me by.

Yeah, I remembered a lot of things, but what I remembered the most was the pain I couldn't leave behind, and it hurt. It always hurt.

I was in Atlanta, Georgia, aboard an American Airlines Boeing headed toward San Francisco, waiting for the plane to take off. I had been among the first to set foot on the plane, so I knew takeoff would take another hour or so. I was going to visit an old friend during the holidays. I did this yearly; it had become a little ritual of mine. It was early in the morning, and I hadn't gotten enough rest the night before.

I would get jittery and bouncy usually on the day of or before I jumped on a plane. I was tired, and the gentleman in front of me kept leaning over. His seat kept reclining, and he kept banging on my tray table. It annoyed me. He must have been in his mid-sixties. He had a snub nose and short gray hair, and his skin looked as if it were worn by the sun. He wore a light brown coat over another even lighter brown coat, and he kept nagging to himself as if he were upset over something. He smelled odd, a distasteful scent, that of old cologne and mouthwash. The smell drove me to the edge of my window seat. I couldn't tolerate it, it was that bad. He slammed back again, this time a little harder than before. I almost fell off my seat. He turned around and took a quick look at me and frowned as if it was my fault, and maybe it was. Lately I was at fault for many things.

"I'm sorry. These seats are made too stiff. I'm just trying to get comfortable, you hear? This is going to be a long flight. The longest I have been on in a long time. You know?" he said rapidly as he reclined his seat some more. Back and forth, side to side, he kept actuating around. His feet slammed against the base of the plane and his arm reached toward the center console of his seat. I said nothing, and I couldn't have. I didn't have enough energy to do so. I smiled and looked out the window. The sun was beginning to peak, and the only thing on my mind was this long tedious flight.

"Yes, it's going to be a long flight," I replied soon afterward. The man turned away, and I leaned my head toward the window again and took a deep breath. My eyes were heavy and my body was exhausted. I wanted to fall asleep, considering the six hours of complete immobility I had before me, but I knew my paranoia would get the best of me in no time. I didn't like flying. I never did. I mean, there was something unsettling about flying. I couldn't relax. I couldn't think correctly, and sometimes I felt as if the very breath in my lungs was being pulled out of me. I think a lot of it had to do with control. For example, if this plane was bound to fail, then I, myself, would have no control over the outcome. Meaning, if I was meant to die, then I was meant to die, and there was nothing anyone could do to prevent that. But of course, this wasn't something you would want to have rattling in the back of your head.

No one ever wants to die, especially not on a plane, but the truth is, what if the plane did decide to fail today? What if today was my time to go? What if every moment in my life had been carefully picked out in order to direct me here? It's hard not to think of this while boarding a plane, and I think a lot of people, if not all, always think of the possibility. "What if I die on this plane?" Well, there's nothing anyone could do about that.

I just didn't trust flying. I didn't trust driving. I didn't trust anything, really, not even myself at times. And now, at twenty-five, I trusted even less than I did before. I'm not sure exactly how I got to this point, but the older I got, the less I trusted the world around me. I guess that was a part of growing up. The more I grew, the less I felt, or maybe it was the other way around. The more I grew, the more I felt, and maybe deep down within me I just ignored everything a little more.

I had become a master at blocking out things, things that shouldn't be blocked out, but that's how my life was: I either took things in or blocked them out completely, and never did I question my natural intuition. I had this keen sense of things, things most people didn't pick up on, and I was usually right about them, but I never listened to myself, and when I did, it was usually too late. In other words, I didn't want to fly, but I did it anyway. I had to; it was the right thing to do.

About fifteen minutes had passed and I was returning to my seat. I went to use the restroom before the flight took off. The plane was somewhat empty, which I found to be odd. Half the seats were unoccupied, and almost everyone on board was asleep or reading a book or had their eyelids cemented on their phones.

It was quiet, a little too quiet, and that alone made me feel even more uneasy. God, I hated this feeling. I was a complete wreck, and the anticipation made me feel as if I was stuck in a time loop, one where I was constantly colliding within myself and snowballing back to the beginning—to crash all over again. What a mess! I couldn't hold it together. Sure, I was quiet sitting on my seat, minding my own business, looking out the window as if I had it all under control, but in all reality, in my head there was so much more. There I played over and over about a thousand different scenarios of how things could possibly go wrong.

But that's how it was. There was always a war in my head, in my heart, and together the two could never come to terms. When it came to matters of the heart, the mind always had a hard time agreeing and vice versa. If one wanted something, then the other would interfere, and by the time another opportunity presented itself, the two would end up with nothing. They were very difficult to align, at least for me, and if I ever had the chance to understand how the two could coexist, then please, by all means, put me first in line, sign me up, because I wasn't afraid to admit that maybe I was a little crazy, that maybe everyone was like this and that maybe everyone was trying to figure themselves out as time went on.

As the minutes gathered, a young flight attendant with gold-spun curly hair, bright eyes, and full red lips entered through the front of the cabin. She was well groomed, well dressed, and very conservative. With a confident smile, she was slowly passing through the aisle, making sure every passenger felt safe and comfortable. Behind her was another flight attendant. She was about the same build. She had tawny, straight red hair, high cheekbones, and thin pink lips. She wore the same dark blue uniform with a little gold pin as the flight attendant before her, and she was pushing a little metal cart filled with beverages and snacks. They both walked in unison and they did so flawlessly.

I always admired people who worked to serve others. In a lot of ways, I found that to be inspiring. Imagine that you had to be another type of person to be able to take people's inconsistencies with a smile, and that was something I knew I couldn't do, at least not in this lifetime. By the time the flight attendants got to me, more passengers had filled the cabin. The aisles were congested, and the chaos of the plane began in a low tone and built to a loud rumble. The air went from a stale smell to a mixture of perfumes and other unwelcome scents. This, too, drove me mad, but I kept my composure. It was no symphony to my nostrils.

It nauseated me, and from the dark corners of my head a continuous thumping emerged from the shadows. I dove back toward the window and placed my hand over my nose as if it was going to help, but obviously it didn't. The commotion seemed endless and defeating.

"Great! What else could go wrong on my not-so-great day already?" I asked myself several times over and over. I gave up. There were many people bumping into one another, bumping into my row and even the gentleman in front of me.

"Can you guys watch it, you hear? I'm already uncomfortable as it is. These darn planes have no legroom. The cushions on the seats are too hard and the armrest is too small," said the gentleman in front of me as he waved to the ocean of people passing through the aisle. His voice was croaky and rough. Maybe he was a smoker, I thought. The parade of loud footsteps and even louder chatter surrounded the plane.

All of this kind of made me wish I could have fallen asleep, but that's how flying was. It wasn't meant to be delightful, and I understood that. In fact, come to think of it, I have never had a good experience flying . . . not even as a child. If I recall correctly, when I was eight, this little girl with freckles and crooked teeth sat in the row in front of my mother and me, and as the flight progressed, my mother insisted that I go and play with her to kill time. I didn't want to, but considering the circumstances, I did so.

This is what I meant when I mentioned my keen intuition, which I should have followed that day, because shortly, the little girl threw up all over me. It's hard to believe I can't remember what came after that. Another unfortunate time was when I was sixteen. That was the first time I'd traveled alone. The first time I felt like an adult. While the experience was meant to be spellbinding, it wasn't. I got on the wrong flight and ended up in Boston. That was a nightmare. I was supposed to go to New York City. I was going to surprise my father for his birthday, but that didn't happen, and of course, it didn't go as planned, as many things in my life have gone, without course and completely intuitively.

Suddenly, I felt someone bump into my row. Every seat connected shook extremely hard, as if someone was trying to lift the seats off their hinges. My head sprang back a little.

"Ouch!" I softly yelled to myself. I turned back and it was a young man, probably in his late twenties. He stood at the edge of my row in the middle of the aisle, hauling three very large multicolored sports bags. I looked around the plane some more. Everyone was beginning to take their seats. I looked at the young man again, and he reminded me of someone. His cheeks were finely chiseled and his jawline was perfectly symmetrical. His eyebrows were bushy and his frame was as firm as marble. His skin was softly tanned, and his hair was messy and untamed. (Not in a bad way.) He wore boot-cut jeans, but he wasn't wearing any boots. He had on a red button down, which was slightly loose, and a black jacket. He looked familiar, but I couldn't put a name to his face.

Maybe I knew him or maybe I didn't. Nonetheless I wasn't going to say anything. He didn't smell odd or off; his scent was just right, or right enough not to push me away. He gazed at his boarding pass, flicked his hand on it, and quickly looked into my eyes. I turned away. I glanced out my window. I wasn't shy; I just didn't like eye contact. There was something about making eye contact that was too intimate to bear. I always believed that there was some kind of exchange when sudden eye contact occurred. I always thought that perhaps the reason why it did occur was that your souls would call out before your eyes even touched. Either way, it was uncomfortable and somewhat intrusive—at least it felt intrusive—and I know that as preposterous as it sounds, I wasn't ready to let some random stranger into my space like that.

"Okay, this is it," he lightly whispered to himself, and then reached behind him to place all three sport bags into the overhead storage. He tapped it open and snuck one bag within the storage cabin, leaving the second one on the available seat next to him. He took another look at me, but this time it was even faster than before. He then sat beside me; there was an empty seat between us and another one next to him where his sport bag rested.

I paid no attention to him and continued to look out the window as I waited for the plane to take off. It had been almost an hour since I had boarded the plane, and now the sun was full and my watch displayed the time of 7:00 a.m. on the dot.

Of course, flights never took off at the time they said they would. There was always something to delay them from taking off, or maybe it was me. Perhaps, in some sense, I brought this on myself. I brought this pessimistic attitude, which led me to a series of unfortunate events. Either way, it didn't matter. My real problem was ahead of me, and I wasn't sure if I was ready to face it once again.

The intercom went on. It was one of the in-flight crew members talking. "Ladies and gentlemen, the captain has turned on the fasten-seat-belt sign. If you haven't already done so, please stow your carry-on luggage underneath the seat in front of you or in an overhead bin. Please take your seat and fasten your seat belt. And also make sure your seat backs and folding trays are in their full upright position. We are expecting to take off within the next thirty minutes." The passengers did so. By now the plane was nearly full and everyone was sitting in their seats for takeoff. I was anxiously waiting for this to happen.

I didn't like takeoffs. I always felt as if I was on a missile rioting itself toward outer space. I know I'm being dramatic, but every time the plane accelerated, for some reason everything inside the cabin moved slower. It was like a dream, as if it wasn't really happening, but it was, and to top it off, every flight was different, and no matter how many times I was on a plane, each time was a different experience, a different outcome, and I would leave with a different perspective every time I set foot off the terminal.

In so many ways, flying was a lot like life. You'd be going somewhere on a specific path, and sometimes you'd fall and the drop didn't necessarily kill you. It just gave you a scare, and from that you'd learn a valuable lesson, one that would teach you to either keep on going down that specific path or find a new one. It was the same idea with people. Some would take you high while others would bury you down deep within the ground, and how you took the experience was based on you.

Everyone was now buckled into their seats. The crowd got really silent as the engines began to roar. Slowly, the plane began to move and my heart began to race. It pounded as if it wanted to be removed from my body. The plane began to catch speed as my face began to wince. This was the part I hated the most. Although I knew what to expect, to me, the entire idea was still foreign. I didn't feel like myself, and as the plane accelerated, I was slightly pushed to the back of my seat as if my body was sinking in a giant cushion made of marshmallows.

"You don't look so well. First timer?" the guy sitting next to me asked, the one with the red shirt and the untamed hair. He smiled as his eyebrows lifted toward the ceiling of the plane.

"No, it's not my first time. I don't feel too well. I don't like flying." I brushed my bangs to the side of my face and bit the tip of my pointer finger's nail.

"I hear you. Well, if it makes you feel any better, I don't like flying either, but I don't like a lot of things. Either way, I have to do it, you know?

"And come to think of it, I don't think anyone really likes flying. Some will say they do, but once they experience a scare, that completely changes. Most officials say it's the safest way to travel, but I have this theory." He paused for a second, then continued to ramble. "The officials say you have a better chance of dying in a car crash than in a plane crash, but I say what if you got on a plane as often as you did a car? Wouldn't that increase your chances of dying on a plane or of something bad happening? The thing is, we don't get on planes as often; let's say two to three times per year as opposed to two to three times per day as we do cars. You know?"

The tip of the plane began to tilt upward. The engines roared even louder, and this swooshing sound surrounded the cabin. I didn't reply, but he did make some kind of sense. If you got on a plane more often, then yes, your risks of an accident were greater. Well, that's obvious. I looked at him; I nodded and held the armrest firmly as my jaw began to tense up. It was as if I was anticipating a needle piercing into my arm, which, by the way, I also dreaded. I closed my eyes, and it wasn't because I was afraid but because as the plane ascended, I was waiting for something terrible to happen. At times my imagination would get the best of me, and clearly this was one of those times.

I cringed, and then I slowly opened my eyes to look out the window. Maybe he did have a point, and as I said earlier, if I was bound to die on this plane, then really, there's nothing anyone could do to stop such a horrible thing from happening. We were no longer on the ground, and the sound from the turbines flew through my ears, through the cabin. The plane was shaking mildly as we ascended some more. The ground was beginning to fade. All the city details began to form an even bigger picture, one I couldn't recognize. It's funny how it's all connected. It's funny how one city leads to another. How one road leads to another. How one secret leads to another. How one friendship leads to another and so on. Everything is connected one way or another, and it's surreal how it all plays out with time.

As the plane leveled out, I began to feel calm. My hands loosened up, and my back began to unwind. I began to feel relaxed, and my breath regulated itself. I felt my weight again, and my heart began to beat at its normal pace, and everything felt as it once had (before I hopped on the plane). Maybe I did overreact. Sometimes I did, and maybe—it was, in fact—the wait that made everything so monumental. It made small problems into big ones. To me, flying was the worst, but once I got into the air, everything wasn't as bad as I'd thought it would be. Maybe it was in my head or maybe it was not, but one thing always remained: flying always brought something out of me. Something old and ignored but never forgotten, something far but near enough to claim me as its own.

I always felt nostalgic looking out the window, watching the wing of the plane slowly surf the clouds and stretch outward toward the horizon. I mean, yes, flying was at times a nuisance to me, but it also reminded me of them. The two people I couldn't forget. The two people who haunted me no matter how far I went, who were always there . . . lurking in the back of my head, in the pit of my heart like old memories demanding attention. I could never ignore them. The two were a part of me, and they represented the parts of me that I, myself, would never be able to understand.

2

"Always remember me." That was something she would say. Every time we parted, she went on for a few seconds about how important it was to remember her, about how important it was to remember this moment. (The ones I shared with her.) She was a bit obsessed with the idea, and I never understood why, and to this day I still don't understand it at all. It was something so simple, yet hard to swallow, and I always thought it was somewhat of a taboo to even say. I mean, ideally no one wants to be forgotten, everyone wants to be remembered one way or another, and no one ever wants to slowly dissolve into the nothingness of another person's mind. So to constantly mention it was something out of the ordinary.

She would say it so much that I myself began to eventually repeat it to her, and because of that, I, too, became paranoid over the idea of becoming a memory as well. (I think a lot of us were.) As strange as it sounds, taking advantage of the moment became one of my intricacies. I never took anything for granted. I always paid attention to details. I always took note of the qualities things had to offer, whether it was music, food, watching a new movie, traveling to a familiar place, or even running into old friends. I always acknowledged the bright side: the good side of things. No matter how dull or dim or dark or bright it was, I always looked for more, because ultimately, there was always more; that is, if you were looking for it.

It's a gift to appreciate such things, and because of that, I always think laughter is a good source, a good foundation to build on. By that I mean that giving someone a great laugh could open up the possibility of them remembering you. To me, that was such a beautiful thing. Imagine that: imagine the perk of being humorously funny all the time as if it were some kind of superpower, some kind of sixth sense.

If that were so, then perhaps she would have not been overly obsessed with being forgotten. Now, I'm not saying she wasn't funny, because at times, well, when she needed to be, she was, but I think a lot of us are like that. I think a lot of us could be amusing and interesting and so much more than we're willing to be. After all, being more than just a memory required work, and it wasn't the kind that came easy or cheap or overnight. No, never that.

It took more than a few good jokes, and I think she knew this as if she had discovered some ancient artifact, some kind of specific knowledge hidden from the light of the world that only she had access to. Perhaps this was why I couldn't forget her. Perhaps this was why every night since then she had haunted me as if she were following me, only to remind me about how I shouldn't forget her or how I should always be remembering her, thinking of her, or whatever it was she intended. Well, she got it done, and accurately, because everywhere I went, no matter where I was, there was always something that took me back, and most of the time it felt like an old car ride taking me home.

What was worse was how sometimes the little things about her manifested themselves in the most surprising of ways, like right then: I was in a plane headed toward San Francisco, and once again I caught myself dwelling in the memory of her. She was just that hard to forget, that easy to remember. The world revolved around her as if she was the sun, and I was just another person completely in love with the way she lit up the sky.

"Sorry about earlier. I got a bit preachy and theological. I usually don't talk much." The voice emerged from the corner near my left ear as I quickly snapped back to the plane ride. I had completely dozed off looking out the window. I did that at times. It was one of my many bad habits. Sometimes, I would get lost in my thoughts, in my little daydreams. I did that too often. My hand glided through my hair as I turned toward the voice.

"I don't think we've officially met. I'm Owen," said the guy sitting next to me as his hand reached out as if I were meant to give him something. Perhaps something I didn't know I had or something I did have but had no clue what to do with. Owen: the name echoed through my body as if each letter contained a shock wave running sharp needlelike stings through my hands and arms and legs. For a brief moment I sat there, unsure. *Of course, he would have the same name as him,* I thought as I paused to think. Of course his memory, too, would follow me around as if it had no other place to go, and last, of course, only these types of things happen to me (literally). I didn't say anything as his hand froze. It stood in midair for a few seconds, shamelessly and without fear of rejection. He smiled as if he were embossed. A few seconds later he tucked his hand back to his side.

"Okay," he said quietly to himself. I didn't reply. "C'mon, you're not going to answer me?" he said sincerely as he smiled slightly again. It was a half smile, the kind you gave when you felt uncomfortable or overly confident. His teeth were barely visible, and his upper lip slowly elevated farther away as if he was meant to open more than just his mouth.

The nerve of him! I didn't have to say anything to him, to anyone. It was a tad arrogant of him to even think that because he asked me a question, he automatically deserved an answer. I mean, yes, I was being a bit rude, but in all reality, I didn't have to answer back. Nonetheless, he did have a good sense of kindness. His smile and gesture gave it away. It radiated out of him like a hot stream on a cold day, and it wasn't that I didn't want to talk to him. I mean, after all, we were stuck on this plane for the next six hours or so, but the other reason why I was so hesitant was that he instantly reminded me of someone, of him, and it was all so sudden, unexpected, and the feeling was like a thousand memories passing through me all at once as if they were trying to squeeze through a keyhole.

I blinked twice, intentionally. I sometimes blinked when I didn't have the words to say. For a few seconds I thought carefully about how to reply. The seconds felt like hours. I wasn't shy. I just wasn't sure if I wanted to engage in a full conversation. To me, once I went in, it was all or nothing, and I wasn't sure if I was ready for that type of commitment. I know, I know, maybe I was being overly dramatic, passive-aggressive, and a little careless. Or maybe I was overthinking it too much, but it's not like any of that mattered anyway. I knew where all of this was going, and it was all beginning to feel familiar.

"I'm Wes," I said softly. I turned away, and then my eyes found themselves back toward Owen. "It's just." I paused again. "You remind me of someone," I said with effort, as if I was pushing the reply out of me, as if my tongue had gotten caught between my teeth and the roof of my mouth was cement-like, making it hard for my words to reach the surface. I grunted, maybe because in the back of my throat, Owen, my Owen, was looking for a way out, but I held him back in. Maybe I should not have said that. Maybe I didn't. Maybe I thought it and thought I said it aloud.

"I remind you of someone? I hope that's not a bad thing." *Shoot! I did say it,* I thought as he smiled again. This time it was almost a full smile. His teeth glowed, and my eyes sparkled a little. I was, indeed, instantly attracted to him, but still, that wasn't enough for me. I wasn't the type of person to throw myself at people just because they reminded me of someone or because I was attracted to them and whatnot. But nonetheless, my eyes gravitated toward Owen, and it was for the wrong reasons, but like all things that randomly came to you out of the blue, they were almost always for the wrong reason, and possibly no reason for them to happen was needed at all.

Good or bad, whatever the reason was, in the end, it meant nothing, at least not for the time being. Besides, almost everything about this Owen reminded me of my Owen. His height, the way he dressed, and the way he made an entrance. Even his smile, scent, and messy hair reminded me of my Owen. I was sure he was his own person, in his own right, but right then I just couldn't help it: everything about this guy reminded me of him. And what I found disturbing was how the very memory of Owen, my Owen, stung even harder each time he found his way through my consciousness, and it hurt some days more than others and other days more than before.

I think I was beginning to feel sorry for myself, because here I was contemplating those two again as I always did when I found myself feeling alone. As I always did when I felt lost between reality and a daydream, between what once was and what still is, but it wasn't always like this. I wasn't always running and chasing and letting go to find myself holding on even tighter. It didn't always hurt. It didn't always feel gut-wrenching, or as if I was drowning in the cold water. In fact, most of the time, it was the opposite. It was all sunshine and bluebirds chirping through the day.

It was sometimes beautiful, and the thought of the two did haunt me, but it wasn't always nightmares and darkness. Gosh, just thinking about them made it feel as if it was a lifetime ago, and maybe it was. It sure felt that way sometimes. It sure felt as if they never existed.

I could still remember the first time I met the two. It was as if it were yesterday. My parents had moved from Illinois to Florida to seek better opportunities. In Illinois, my father was working as a night counselor for Morton College and my mother was a stay-at-home mom.

At the time, before we moved, we lived in Bridgeview, which was in Chicago. This was in the early nineties. Things were different back then— things meant so much more. Like when you met someone for the very first time, it actually did do something to you. And I wasn't sure what it was, but I knew it was always something that felt real, something that brought out a thousand different sides of you. Some old, some new, and sometimes a new friendship moved you in ways you couldn't comprehend.

When we moved to Florida, we went all the way south. My mother wanted to make a new life in the Florida Keys, but my father was guaranteed a position at Miami Dade College. He was an associate professor, and my mother landed a gig in the local SunTrust Bank. At the time, I attended Sunset Park Elementary, but that was not where I met Owen. We had moved to Kendall, to a little community called Four Quarters. There were only six buildings in the community, and a handful of old people filled each of them. The buildings looked old, the parking lots looked old, and it smelled old too. Each building had two stories. The first floor had one-bedroom apartments, and the second floor had two- to three-bedroom apartments. Other than the old people and the old-looking buildings, it was a pretty decent accommodation.

In Chicago, we lived in a much bigger place, but it was half empty. Not a lot of people lived there, but somehow I still managed to make some friends. There we lived in a one-story house with a white fence, a large yard, and some extra land, lots of land, filled with trees. Of course, some would say that moving to Miami was a downgrade for us. Yes, we went from a three-thousand-square-foot house to a seven-hundred-square-foot apartment that was too old to even describe. In other words, it wasn't paradise, it didn't have quite the view, nor did it fulfill my expectations of Miami, but—and there is always a giant "but" in the middle somewhere— nonetheless, we were thankful. We were together, and we were alive and well; not to mention, we were happy.

It took about five months to finally settle in. I was just turning ten years old, and summer was right around the corner. Almost every day while living in Chicago I rode my bicycle after school as long as I was within visible distance. My mother would sit out by the porch and watch me do circles with some friends in the parking lot. It wasn't necessarily the most exciting thing to do, but when you're a kid, anything beats being inside the house.

In Miami it was a little bit different. There were absolutely no kids playing outside in Four Quarters, and with summer catching up behind me, I began to wonder what was going to become of it. Every summer in Chicago was special. Every summer left a mark on my soul. It was magical. There's something special about summer. Something that's hard to explain, but you could feel the difference in the air. You feel it fill your lungs, and the difference tingles through your skin. And that summer, the very first summer in Miami, was beginning to feel as if maybe this summer wasn't going to be like the last. I began to think maybe this summer would be dull and slow and quiet and lonely, not to mention boring. That summer I began to think how maybe this summer wouldn't give me something to remember.

That year, as the school term ended, every day I did my homework and sat by the window as if I was waiting for something to happen, maybe even a miracle. For those first five months nothing happened. No other kids appeared, and I just sat by the window on a daily basis. I sat there day in and day out, wondering if moving here had been a mistake. Through rain and sunshine I thought this, and as summer approached, I had almost lost all hope of making a neighborhood friend.

Then the school term ended, and a few days into summer a miracle happened. Out of the blue, a young boy on a neon-orange rally bicycle appeared. Every day I saw him ride his bicycle, and every day I asked my mother if it was okay for me to go outside. She said no each time, and I never understood why. I mean, I would go out every day back in Chicago, and now, here, I was restricted. I had laws, and if I didn't abide by them, then who knew what my mother was capable of.

Every day I saw this boy, and every day I just wanted to jump on my bicycle and chase him. You know, kid stuff. Then on the twelfth day of summer, another miracle happened. My mother finally let me out as if she had been waiting for me to allow myself out, or so it seemed, because at the edge of my anticipation, by the time I was about to break down of boredom, she just let me out. She let me go outside as long as I was within a viewable distance.

It's funny when you're a kid how even the slightest little thing can mean the world to you. How something as simple as going outside can change your entire life. How one day can shift eternity and make things go as if they were meant to go. What I'm trying to say is, if that day hadn't happened, if my mother hadn't let me out, then perhaps my life would have been different and the outcome of it all wouldn't have been the same. I wonder.

I cracked open the door, lifted my yellow bicycle toward the first floor, and began to pedal near the boy. His gray Nike Air Max shoes were worn, and his shirt was big enough to fit three of him. I remember this because it was the first thing I said when I spoke to him. I rode a little closer as I looked back toward my apartment window. My mom was sitting there watching me.

She waved as if she wanted me to go and talk to him. I nodded, and then I smiled and went on my way. I got close enough. The back of his shirt was sweaty, and his ears were really red. The day was hot, too hot, perhaps even the hottest it was that year.

"That's a really big shirt," I said as I trailed behind him as if I knew I was meant to follow this boy for the rest of my life. He stopped his bicycle and looked back.

"You're still on training wheels?" he said as if he was surprised. I had only been riding my bicycle for a little over two years, and yes, some would say that it was completely absurd that my ten-year-old self was still on training wheels, but sometimes I was a slow learner. The kids back home used to make fun of me, but it was always in good fun.

"Yes, I just started riding three nights ago and my father is going to teach me how to ride without them. So for now these will do," I said with enthusiasm. I was really excited to be outside, and of course that was a lie. I just didn't want to make an awful impression. Thing is, when you're young, the first impression is literally everything. I didn't want to make it seem as if I was a baby. At a young age I understood how in this life, first impressions were the difference between life and death and how one bad impression could ruin everything, let alone haunt you for the rest of your life. I wasn't ready to end this friendship before it even began.

"Oh, okay, well, I'm Owen, and this is my older brother's T-shirt," he said as he cranked on his pedal and led the way.

"I'm Westlyn, but you can call me Wes. My parents call me Wes."

"Wes? Like North, South, East, West?" Owen murmured.

"Yes, exactly, but without the *t*," I said firmly. I didn't want to set myself up for cheesy jokes, although I had fallen victim to several back home. It was somewhat of a norm for me.

"Okay, cool," he replied with the color of friendship smeared on his eyes, and that was the beginning of something unexpected. The beginning of what I had been looking for since we moved to Florida. It's funny how things work. It's funny how sometimes you do get what you ask for and maybe not in an instant. Maybe not the night after, but eventually, if you keep on believing, then the universe does have a way of responding to you and it doesn't forget. What you ask for eventually comes for you, and when it does, it appears to you to remind you of how important you are, because in all honesty I was; at least that's how I like to see it.

A few months had passed, and Owen and I really grew into each other's lives. There was something unusual about this boy, and since the first day we met, I was pulled in. I couldn't put my finger on it. I was intrigued by him, by his genuine character and charismatic appeal.

Every day we played outside, and sometimes my mother and father would allow him to play cards with me in our living room where my mother always made us lunch and sometimes even invited him for dinner. In a lot of ways, Owen was the friend I had always wanted. That summer we spent countless nights talking on the phone, learning more about each other and about all the things we loved.

Our friendship really bloomed, and from there on out, it was as if he was the only person who understood me. I mean, he knew things about me and I knew things about him, and together we shared our childhood. Those were the days, the good ones, the ones I always came back to when I needed a reminder of how somewhere out there in the vastness of the earth there was someone who understood me and possibly still loved me for who I was.

About a year later, the following summer, Owen and I were out in the community pool. Sometimes my mother took both of us during the summer. It was then that she came into our lives, and she came like a soaring comet and landed with such force before us. We couldn't ignore her. We were instantly drawn to her for reasons unknown.

"Who's that?" Owen asked as he tried to sit on his basketball beneath the water. I looked back and swam toward the edge of the pool to see who he was talking about. All the other children in the pool were kicking and screaming and yelling as if it were the end of the world. (That year a handful of other kids flourished.) It was a young girl, about our age. She was wearing a black-and-yellow Nirvana T-shirt and a pair of lime-green Wayfarer sunglasses. She was carrying a box filled with books and magazines; we knew this because she dropped some as she walked by. Her hair was black and her skin was very pale. She had dark lipstick on.

She was cool, or at least we thought she was. By this time all the other kids noticed her. She had this distinct look, as if she was not from this place, and it was obvious that she wasn't from Miami, let alone Florida. I don't know; she just didn't seem like she was.

She looked at us as she passed by. She didn't flinch or smile or wave. She gave off this "I don't want to be friends" vibe, and I think, at the time, that's why we were so intrigued by her. She looked again. It was a quick stare down.

"I don't know. Maybe we should talk to her?" I said as a group of kids splashed next to me.

"Yeah, maybe one day we'll catch her outside, but for now let's just keep things the way they are. Maybe adding a new person to our circle can be dangerous, a bad thing, you know?" said Owen as the mysterious girl walked into her apartment. And maybe he did have a point. Sometimes having more friends was indeed something to be proud of, but sometimes it wasn't, for sometimes the more people you knew, the harder it was to let them go. I knew a thing or two about saying good-bye, and it was never an easy task to do. That, and also, having more friends only made you more vulnerable. By that I mean, the more people knew about you, then perhaps the worse it was.

"No, it's not necessarily a bad thing. It's just a little too much for me right now and a little bit haunting, but never mind me. I'm beginning to sound like a crazy person," I said as I looked out the window. I slowly came back to the plane ride and the guy next to me. I was beginning to feel a bit nostalgic about everything I had just thought about.

You know, old feelings and even older memories did that to me. They took me back, they made both good and bad times seem beautiful as if they had never happened and I made them up in my head. They made me realize how some things are meant to be remembered. They made me appreciate what once was even more, and because of them, the two I couldn't forget, I tried to live a little more than the night before.

"Well, either way, it's nice to meet you, Wes," Owen said as both of his arms reached toward the ceiling of the plane. He yawned and slightly slouched back on his reclining seat. By this time the plane was well over 40,000 feet. It was gliding through the air, cutting clouds, and when I looked down, all I saw were colors. There were no cityscapes, no city lights, no city noise, no smells, or anything that reminded me of home. In many ways, I hated flying, but also, in many ways, I enjoyed the fact that I could ideally go anywhere in the world and without questioning. *I could be anywhere in the world right now,* I thought as I sat by the window. And then, I began to think about her. I began to think of her unfulfilled fascination with traveling. She always had this overwhelming desire to leave, and it's funny because that's how we somewhat met her, I remember.

We were sitting out back by the stairs in one of the Four Quarters apartment complexes. Our bikes were thrown on the pavement and we were discussing where we would want to travel when we got older. Owen was throwing a baseball toward the sky and catching it with his bare hands. The sound of his hand slamming against the baseball made me cringe. I remember this day because one, I got hit in the face with his baseball, and two, we met her. The girl we saw moving into the community that one day while being in the pool. We were sweating, hungry, and exhausted from riding our bikes for several hours.

"Do you ever feel like you're meant for more?" I said as Owen continued to throw his baseball into the air.

"What feeling?"

"I don't know," I said to Owen.

"Like not growing up here? Like going away to college? Like that?" he replied.

"Well, yes and no. I mean, what if I wasn't meant to be here? What if you aren't meant to be here?" I said, using a flat tone. We were sitting on the stairs waiting for my mother to finish cooking lunch.

"If you hadn't come, I wouldn't have met you," said Owen.

"Yeah," I said as my mood switched. I was beginning to question my eleven-year-old existence; I was perhaps even having a childhood identity crisis. Owen stopped throwing his ball and looked me dead in my eyes.

"What's wrong, Wes? You okay?" His voice was penetrating. His words always had a way of entering. I sometimes felt bad for Owen because from time to time I made him go through things, unnecessary things, too, things that would stress him and sometimes cause an argument between us.

"C'mon, Wes, cheer up," said Owen as he threw his baseball up in the air again.

"Yeah," I replied, and in that moment, another miracle happened. We heard a door crack open, and to our knowledge the sound was loud enough to hear but low enough to be ignored. We both turned our heads and it was her. She was coming out of her apartment, and then, it just hit me. Owen's baseball came raging down like a bat out of hell. A loud pop was heard, and soon after, I screamed and then I began to cry.

My hand and Owen's were firmly pressed over my left eye. I didn't know what to do other than hysterically scream as if I was yelling for my life. I know, again I was being overly dramatic, but like I said, it was meant to happen, because a few moments later, that girl, Harper, came running to our aid with an ice pack. That day something magical happened, another summertime miracle, and it was as if fate decided to let her in, because after that day the three of us were inseparable. After that day there was no one else but us, and it stayed like that for a very long time. Everything was too good to be true.

3

At the beginning of the second hour of flight I began to doze off. I was tired; the exhaustion from waiting to get aboard the plane had caught up to me. I barely kept my eyes open. I was in and out of sleep the same way I was in and out of my thoughts. The older gentleman in front of me was snoring so loud that you'd think he'd swallowed a batch of fireworks. He was loud enough to wake at least two city blocks. It was a little obnoxious of him, but I dealt with it, because on the bright side, things could have been a lot worse by now. Owen, the guy in my row, was asleep, and the rest of the plane was at ease. There was very little movement.

It was 8:32 in the morning and I was eagerly waiting for one of the stewardesses to pass by so I could ask for a cup of coffee. I needed it, and I figured if I stayed awake the entire time, then I would just crash as soon as the plane landed in San Francisco. To me, it made more sense to finally fall asleep on land rather than on a plane where deep down inside I didn't feel too safe. Besides, five more hours to go didn't necessarily feel too bad or too long. I also knew that by the time I got on the plane, I would be landing soon after.

Sometimes getting off a plane was just as fast as getting on it. In a lot of ways, flying was a lot like life, well, my life. I would get on a plane and before I knew it, I was already landing. And it was the same way for almost everything. If I got a new job, by the time I realized an entire year had passed by, I was quitting. It was the same way with people, at least it was for me. One second I was meeting someone and the next second they were gone. The beginning and the end, all cycling around me at once, and not to be melodramatic, but in the end, nothing would last. Nothing would stay. Not this plane ride. Not this moment, not the older gentleman in front of me, nothing. Nothing was meant to be forever.

A little turbulence vibrated the plane. It shook from wing to wing as I looked outside the window. The plane felt as if it suddenly lost altitude. My heart dropped, and my eyes and heart fell toward the floor. I hated when this happened. Almost everyone froze, while the rest of the passengers stayed as they were. The gentleman in front of me woke up in a riot. He lifted his arms and looked toward his right and then toward his left.

"These goddamn flights!" he lashed. "I'm sick and tired of them! All of them!" he said to himself and he moved around his seat to find comfort. I shook myself off and turned on the television screen attached to the seat in front of me. To my surprise they were playing *Jingle All the Way*, the film with Arnold Schwarzenegger and Sinbad. I loved that movie. It reminded me of my childhood, as many things did and as many things have done recently.

I never quite understood this, but when I was a child, I wanted to be an adult so bad, I couldn't wait for the day I became one, and now that I am an adult, I wish I could go back and be a child, even if it's only for one night. Back then the holidays felt so real. Everything about them had such magnitude, and every moment would hit me like a wild boomerang soaking with life, filled with all the things I needed to breathe. Those were the days, the golden days, the ones that defined me. I'm not saying these days are terrible days; it's just that when I was a child, things were a lot less complicated and a lot more fun. I missed that.

I looked toward my left and saw Owen open his eyes. He leaned forward and looked directly at me. "How long was I out? I tend to sleep through these flights, you know." He yawned. "Was I asleep for a long time? What time is it?" he tittered in a low, gruff voice as he looked at his wrist for the time.

"Not too long," I whispered as I turned the television screen off. I smiled as if I was shy, but clearly I wasn't. That gesture was something I did when I didn't know what else to express.

"So, Wes." He cleared his throat. "Tell me about yourself. Where are you from?" He leaned back into his seat, looking at the stewardess heading our way. She was attending the passengers through every aisle. I guess she was making sure everyone on board was comfortable.

"Happy Holidays. Is everything okay with the two of you? Can I get either of you something?" she whispered in a cheerful tone as she interrupted Owen. She had on a different uniform from the other stewardess I saw when I first set foot on the plane. She was wearing a full-sleeve white business shirt with a red tie. She had on the same little shiny gold pin. Her hair was picked up in a bun, and her skin looked soft, so soft that it was indeed questionable. She seemed young with her flushed red cheeks and full cherry lips. She was eighteen, maybe? Perhaps even nineteen, who knew. Owen and I looked toward the edge of the aisle. We said nothing as we looked at each other as if we held a secret, then we looked back at the stewardess.

"Yes, may I have a cup of coffee? With cream and two sugars, but please don't add and mix them in; just give everything to me separately. Please," I said firmly. Last thing I needed was a terrible cup of coffee. That alone could have taken this from an okay situation to a miserable one. Sometimes all it took was a cup of coffee: a good one could steer you in the right direction, and a bad one could make the graves appear closer than they really were.

"Right away, and for you? Can I get you anything, sir?" The stewardess's eyes sank into Owen's eyes as the plane shook slightly again. I looked at Owen and then at the stewardess. She didn't even flinch. She was so casual about the turbulence. I, on the other hand, was not. Every time the plane moved, I moved and in such a way that I found to be disturbing. It was as if I were a small dinghy deserted in the middle of a storm, a terrible one. The stewardess stood there as Owen thought about what he wanted. He paused as if he had a menu in front of him.

I looked at the stewardess with a blank face as he thought about what he wanted. I looked at her hands, hips, and feet for no reason at all just because she was in front of me. I needed coffee. I was feeling drowsy. I wanted to sleep, but this plane, everything about this flight, made it impossible to relax, because I knew the moment I closed my eyes, the plane would shake and each time with more force than before. It was either that or the older gentleman in front of me, with his moving around and snoring; that alone made resting impossible as well. I was annoyed. It was as if God or some kind of higher power was playing a cruel joke on me, taunting me with sleep, picking at me, having a good time as I sat here immobile and miserable.

"Yeah, make that two, but you could mix mine up. I'm okay with that," Owen muttered.

"Right away," said the stewardess. She gave us a big smile and continued to walk down the aisle. She was sweet; I liked her. It was cold inside the plane. Almost everyone sitting near a window had the shade down. It was dim, not too dark inside, but there wasn't enough light coming into the cabin, and I think that's what made the plane even colder. My window shade was one of the very few that was open.

"So, like I was saying, tell me about yourself. Where are you from?" Owen demanded with a touch of curiosity dangling from his eyes, mouth, and ears. I wasn't sure where this was going. I wasn't even sure how to answer that. I know it was a simple question that demanded a simple answer, but like I said, I was exhausted, and talking just made me feel even more exhausted, and the plane's temperature wasn't helping, and it being so damn dim did nothing to keep me afloat as well. I took a deep breath, not in a disturbed way but more in an "I wish I wasn't on this plane" kind of way. I took another deep breath.

"Originally I'm from Chicago, but that was so long ago." I chose my words carefully. And it did feel like it was a lifetime ago, that is, Chicago and what I'd left behind there. Sometimes it even felt as if it wasn't real because as time went on, I had this perception about how sometimes, the furthest memories would feel as if they had never happened, as if they were a dream.

"I've been living in Atlanta for two years, and before that I was living in Miami, Florida, for maybe a little over thirteen years. I grew up there so I like to say I'm from there, but I'm not. Have you ever been there? To Miami?"

"Miami, yes, yes, I have. It's nice there. I was just there about two years ago. Great weather, food, people, and music. I was there for the music festival," he added.

"Yeah, it's nice when you're visiting, but when you live there, it's a different story, you know?" I said as my fingers found themselves. I smiled. I was trying to be nice as if at this time it meant anything, which clearly it didn't. I ignored his music festival comment. I had never been to that event. Once a year the city of Miami would host this music festival, and I hated it because the traffic was out of this world.

"Yeah, I know what you mean. Like when you go on vacation somewhere, let's say, San Francisco, for example. While you're there, you're like, 'Wow, I would love to live here,' but it's only because you're experiencing new things, things you're not used to seeing and doing. So yeah, I get you. The first time you see the Golden Gate Bridge, it's as if you have seen Jesus in the flesh. Then you see the bridge again and again and again, and it somewhat becomes the norm. It goes to be unappreciated no matter how important it once was initially. The same way, people," he paused to clear his throat. I was impressed. For a guy I'd just met, he really seemed to know what he was talking about.

"People oversee people. Experience oversees experiences. And it's all the same. You know?" he continued.

"Yeah." I said and gently laughed, and nodded. To my surprise, that was the same exact way I saw things. Sometimes you became so used to things—that is, people, places, and even things you did on a daily basis, like work or study, and so on—that you completely oversee them for what they once were. You ignore them and just don't pay attention to them as you once did when you first discovered them. I'm not sure if that's how it was for everyone, but for me, growing up and even sometimes now, I tend to take almost all my daily activities for granted.

Owen began to smile, and then he looked at me with this look. This sort of "we understand each other" look. It was this faraway but close enough kind of feeling, and I couldn't explain it, but in that very moment, I didn't feel alone. I felt understood in a strange "I don't know you but I do" kind of way. It felt good, that is, meeting someone and them having somewhat of the same point of view I had.

We continued with the conversation. Owen carried it as if our interaction was a crucial part of his life. His eyes were glued to mine, and it was obvious how interested he was in me. I'm not saying I wasn't, but it was clearly something I didn't want to show and tell. Besides, I didn't need another fling. At the moment, I just needed a friend, someone to talk to, and someone to keep me distracted from all the troubles that were going on in my head. And right now he was it. Maybe he was the right person at the right time.

"So what's a Floridian girl doing all by herself on a flight to San Francisco during a holiday? Seeing family?" His voice was rather pleasant. I hadn't really paid any attention to it until now. I enjoyed the way his thoughts curved out of his mouth. They almost sounded like music, a symphony of words. He kept me amused, on my feet, but anything could have amused me for the time being. Anything could have dazzled me in such a way that I would have remembered it for years to come. In a lot of ways, I recently felt like I wasn't myself and anyone could have filled the void.

"No, it's more complicated than that," I replied as I looked out the window again. I had this thing I did, where I would release pieces of myself, then turn away. I don't know why I was like this; it was just something I had picked up as a child.

"Here you go." Suddenly, the same stewardess returned with a metal rolling cart and our coffees. She stood beside us as she cautiously placed our cups in our cup holders, delicately humming "Jingle Bells."

"Thank you," said Owen as she placed everything else on our tray tables. My thank-you shortly followed. Soon after she faded into the background to attend the other passengers; she was still humming "Jingle Bells" as she walked away.

My coffee was steaming. This was exactly what I needed early in the morning. Like I said, sometimes coffee was a lifesaver. It would pull me out of the grave and direct me toward the light. In other words, it gave me wings, second chances, and sometimes the energy I needed to get things done the right way.

"Complicated, huh? Boyfriend?" asked Owen as he took a sip from his coffee. The plane jolted a little.

"This turbulence is making me uneasy," I said as I held my coffee high so it wouldn't spill over me. "It's complicated." I frowned as I ended the theme and quickly changed the subject. I didn't want to get into my personal business with someone I'd just met. To be honest, it wasn't his business, and although he did have a good vibe, I wasn't used to opening up that easily and that quickly.

For me, things like that took time, a lot of time, even years maybe. He, too, noticed my sudden mood shift and swiftly changed the subject quicker than my frown did when he asked. He began to talk about the reason why he was on the plane. I didn't ask him. I just listened.

"Well, I'm going to visit my sister. She just moved to the city, near Union Square. Is this your first time in San Francisco?" He took another sip off his coffee as I did as well. It was warm and just perfect for the below-zero temperature within the plane, or so it felt.

"No, I've been here three times before. This is my fourth. I usually come out here during the holidays, just for a day or two." I considered. I didn't want to get into it, but something inside of me was telling me to. I wanted to vent without sounding too dramatic as I did at times. I wanted to vent about everything even if it was with a stranger. I wanted to talk about it, about them and why I was running, what had me running, and about where I was running to. I didn't know what I was doing, but I knew deep down inside it was all for something. I just couldn't see it, but it ultimately felt like something was there.

Of course, I didn't say any words. I didn't want to be one of those crazy young women who at any given moment takes advantage of her listener. Besides, imagine how that could come off. I mean, he asked me a simple question about my travels to San Francisco, and I just completely ignore it and jump into my life's troubles? Crazy. Crazy. Crazy.

"It's just," I blurted. I wasn't sure what I was doing. "Sometimes, I go to San Francisco to leave, to escape, you know? And San Francisco is the only place where I can feel like myself again. I sort of get recharged every time I go." The words brawled out of me as if they had been pounding at my guard all week, all month. Of course, I was at my tipping point.

Anyone carrying so much weight on their shoulders was bound to have a tipping point, one they could no longer hold on to. Things were just that complicated, and maybe I was that one crazy lady on the plane.

"You okay?" Owen sputtered as my eyes felt as if they were going to let go. I wanted to cry but I didn't. I held it in as Harper's face flashed before my eyes, her crying sad face, that is, the first time I saw her cry. Sometimes her face would randomly manifest itself, like an old film reel playing at the back of my memory, and every time it did, it broke me to pieces, it shattered things in me, things I didn't even know I had obtained until that one terrible day. That's the thing about best friends. They made you realize how big you were, how small you were, and sometimes, they made you feel as if you didn't exist at all. And going through certain experiences with them just made all the difference. When your best friends are sad, then you're sad as well, and because of that you feel what they feel, and never do you say a word to comfort what you already know.

It was August 12, her thirteenth birthday. She didn't have many friends; therefore she didn't have a traditional birthday. She had what we called a get-together. A get-together was like any other day, but the only difference was, we snuck in beer or anything else we could get our hands into. We would lock ourselves in her room while listening to loud rock music. It was cool. It was the three of us, her mother, and two of her aunts celebrating Harper's birthday in her apartment.

Of course, there were no balloons, no cake, and no birthday-like theme. No one was there—just a bunch of drunk old women listening to Barry Manilow. The entire day Harper went on and on about how her father was supposed to make a cameo. All day she kept talking about how perfect he was, about how much he meant to her, about how great he was, about how he would take her on adventures. When she spoke of him, she was happy. In fact, I had never seen her light up the way she did when she spoke of him. It made me smile, watching her smile, but I think deep down inside she was sad because her parents had been separated all her life. But nonetheless that didn't stop her father from seeing her. He would visit her monthly, and he always made an effort to do so. But this time it was different. This time things didn't go as planned. Of course, her father never showed, and of course, Owen and I witnessed the worst come out of her and it was something no child should ever have to go through, especially not alone.

We were all sitting on her bed in her locked room when suddenly, she lifted herself from the bed and walked toward the door without saying a word. Owen and I looked at each other. We didn't know what she was doing or about to do, but it did come off scary, nerve-wracking, and unpredictable.

"He's not coming." She stood still in front of the door as we sat on her bed behind her. She began to breathe heavily.

"Maybe he'll still make it. We don't know, you know?" I shot enthusiasm in the dark, hoping maybe that would comfort her a little. It didn't, and I think nothing could have. She was in a dark place, and no matter what I said, nothing could have brought her back that night. I felt terrible. I wanted to hold her and tell her it was all going to be okay, but who was I to do such a thing during such a sad time for her? In other words, nothing could have made her feel better, not Owen and especially not me.

"No, it's okay. He's not coming." She paused, and then began to sob. It began with one tear, and then it ultimately turned into an ocean of tears like an unbroken spell and we were there to witness her rain. We rushed toward her and gave her a hug. It was the only thing we could have done, and in that moment, she cried profusely. It was as if our hug had given her the permission she needed to let go and she did, and she didn't know where to hide her tears. They just kept falling with such enormous intensity.

I had never seen someone cry with such passion; in fact, I had never seen someone let down to that extent. She almost vomited. Her eyes were closed and so were mine. I couldn't see. All I did was listen and hug even tighter. It hurt me, seeing her this way. It hurt me, watching one of my best friends feel the burn of disappointment. It made me realize how my problems were just as small as a grain of sand.

Her tears smeared all over my shirt. She continued to sob as we held each other silently. We didn't have the words to ease her down. She just kept breaking apart as if a part of her had died, and maybe it had. Maybe a part of her did shatter into the unknowns, where no light dwelled. Maybe that was the day that changed her. Maybe I could have done more, but I didn't, and maybe if I had known what to do, she would have stayed.

"He forgot about me. He forgot my birthday. I can't believe he did. I can't," she said repeatedly as she tried to calm and collect herself.

"Promise me one thing," she mumbled. "Promise to never forget me. Promise to always remember me no matter what!" She sobbed as I began to sob, and soon afterward Owen began to sob as well. I felt her and a part of me died a little that night, and it was the part I had been saving for someone special. That part now belonged to Harper, and that night it never came back to me. It just faded into the night, and the worst part was, I think I was okay with never seeing it again.

And that was how it all began. That's how her "always remember me" speech came about, the one she would say every time we went our separate ways for the day. It was because of her father and how he never showed beyond that point. How he never returned to her. She spent her entire childhood wondering what had happened to him, why he had disappeared, why he never bothered to call.

She never got a proper explanation or an answer, not from her mother or relatives or even us. We would all change the subject as soon as the thought manifested itself. It became forbidden, a subject we all avoided at all cost, because we just didn't know how to handle it. We didn't know why, and it wasn't because we were too young; it was just one of those things. It was one of those things that you'd probably never quite understand.

Eventually, as the years passed, she got over it, or so I thought, but every time her birthday was near or the holidays were right around the corner, you could see a slight hurting pulsating from the centers of her eyes. You could see this silent call for help radiating from her broken smile. She was brave. I mean, I always knew her father suddenly vanishing ate her alive, but she continued to smile, she continued to laugh, and she continued to live as if nothing bothered her at all. And because of that, I did make the promise she asked me to make no matter how distant we became. No matter what life threw at me. I kept my word, and since that day I never forgot her. No matter how much I tried to, she was always there. She had become my star, and I was just another person in love with the way she lit the night sky.

4

I stood up from my seat to stretch. My left leg was beginning to go numb and both of my arms felt stiff. I had to get up. Sitting down for so long made me anxious and electric, and the two cups of coffee I had back to back weren't helping either. They really gave me a surge, one I wasn't expecting. By this time my drowsiness had diminished and all I was left with was this upbeat spark of energy that rang all over. It was beyond my body. I was jittery and anxious.

I sat back down on my seat, looked out the window, and sighed. Owen was in the restroom and many of the passengers were awake. The cabin now was full of light and chatter. There were children playing aboard the plane and all the stewardesses were in full effect, rolling back and forth into the aisles with refreshments and snacks. Since I got on the plane they were always in high spirits, which I found to be pleasant but not surprising. That was one thing you couldn't take away from flying. Every plane I had ever been on had an amazing crew. They were highly attentive, and they always paid attention to the details. But they had to be that way.

I, on the other hand—if I worked here, I would have been the complete opposite. I would have been lazy. I would have dragged my feet down the aisle and I would probably have been annoyed with everyone. Imagine that: a train wreck working as a stewardess. Ha! Wouldn't that be a sight to remember?

"Would you like a chicken sausage Danish combo?" one of the stewardesses offered. She was pushing a squeaky cart filled with sandwiches.

"No, that's okay. I'm not hungry," I said.

"Okay, dear, just let me know if you change your mind," she murmured as I nodded. We exchanged smiles and continued to do what we were doing. She placed a Danish wrapped in plastic, a bag of chips, and a can of club soda on Owen's table and left. I held off on the snacks because I didn't drink soda and I never liked plane food. To me, everything tasted stale and leftover, like old bread: hard to chew and difficult to swallow. I couldn't give in to it, I wouldn't, although I was beginning to feel a few rumbles coming from the pit of my abdomen. Yes, I was hungry, but there was no way I was going to eat what they offered.

The idea of it made me want to gag, and it was something I knew I wouldn't have considered, no matter how starved I was. This was no disrespect to the crew, but I had to admit, the food was questionable.

About ten minutes later Owen arrived from the restroom. He pulled his hands out of his pockets as he sat down in his seat. He sighed as his brawny body rested against the chair. He then moved his neck in a circular motion as if he were stretching it. His bones cracked, they made a snapping sound one by one, and it was gross.

"The restrooms are really clean. Did you know that?" he whispered as he leaned toward me.

"Yes, I know." I giggled lightly to myself. I thought it was funny how out of all the things, that was the first thought that ran through his mind as he sat back down. It was random, he was random, and in a strange, unfolding kind of way I was attracted to it all.

"No, really, for an airline restroom it's spotless. I was washing my hands and I saw my reflection on the floor, on the toilet, on the ceiling, and on the walls," he asserted. He was firm about it. Maybe he was serious, too. I couldn't tell and I didn't want to argue with him. I just quietly laughed within myself because it was ridiculous.

"What's this?" he asked, looking at the array of food on his table.

"It's the spectacular chicken sausage Danish combo and a drink." My sarcasm filled our aisle.

"Oh, all right." He went into the bag and pulled out the wrapped Danish. He carefully opened it like a letter in a clean envelope. He went for his first bite.

"This is great," he said, savoring his first bite. "You didn't get one of these?" He bent toward his plate and resumed.

"No, I wasn't feeling it. Something about it didn't add up," I explained. I didn't want to sound like a downer. After all, he was enjoying his meal, and I didn't want to encourage any thoughts about how his food wasn't really food, good food, that is.

"Do you ever miss your hometown?" he randomly asked with a mouthful.

"Hmm, I'm not sure. Why do you ask?" For a moment I was confused about his question. Maybe he had a bag of skeletons in his closet. Or maybe he was just like me. Maybe he just wanted someone to talk to, as I did. Someone to ask me something, anything, really. I don't know. I was hesitant, but I was also delighted to see where this was going, and to be honest, I wasn't sure why. Maybe it was the coffee rush or maybe it was something else, but one thing was for sure: I was beginning to feel a little more comfortable than before.

And as the seconds accumulated, Owen seemed less and less threatening and more and more like someone I would have known. Like someone I was willing to be friends with. I hadn't had this feeling in a while. Overall, he wasn't intrusive; he was just a guy wanting to talk to a girl about things that mattered. That is, to him and maybe even to me, and like I mentioned before, things could have been worse. I could have sat next to a situation, a real problem. By that I mean, someone who could have made the flight worse instead of easier. Fate has a funny way of showing itself, and maybe Owen was here to calm me down for what was bound to come.

"I don't know," he mentioned as he crumpled the plastic the Danish was in. "Just thinking out loud maybe," he added. He popped open his soda using his pointer finger and began to take big gulps as if he hadn't drank any liquids in the past few days. I didn't say a word. He then caught his swallow as if he wanted to say something, perhaps something important that he himself had been harboring inside. He opened his mouth, but it wasn't to take another gulp. He then hesitated, and all this time I thought I was the only one who would initiate a conversation to unexplainably shut it down before it even began. He looked at his soda can and then he looked at me, flinching.

Then I did something I hardly ever did. "Where are you from?" I asked. "I don't think you've told me." The question flowed out of me. I wasn't the type to ask questions. It was usually the other way around. All my life I had been like this. All my life I was the one answering questions instead of asking them.

"I'm from Charlotte, North Carolina." The mood suddenly shifted, and I wasn't sure which direction it shifted to, but nonetheless it was a direction where the two of us felt a little more comfortable, or so it seemed. He smiled and then I smiled. The cabin was loud, but it felt as if only he and I were on board this plane. If felt as if we had magically vanished into our own little world. And it was a world that seemed a little too familiar for me.

"I was just thinking about my sister, since she moved out not so long ago and I was wondering if she ever missed home. I still live at home with my parents. So I'm just wondering, you know? She doesn't really call or anything like that, and I pretty much invited myself over because she hadn't invited any of us to visit her in San Francisco yet." For a second he looked puzzled. I paused for a moment as well and thought about it. I thought about why people did that to begin with. By that I mean, not call loved ones and sometimes ignore them.

"I think everyone who leaves home misses it one way or another," I said.

"And I think no matter how far you go, eventually you do return home—all of us do. But I don't know. I mean, it's different for everyone, but trust me when I tell you. So, yes, I'm also sure she does miss home. There's no doubt about it, but leaving is part of growing up. I mean, I miss my hometown too. It's where I grew up, you know? And I miss the little things even more." I began to chuckle as I continued. "Like the things you take for granted, like the people and some of the places you see every single day. Like the ocean and the weather. You know, the little things. So yeah, don't dwell on it too much. She's probably busy. *Really* busy, you know?"

For once, I did have a good answer and I felt as if I knew where he was coming from. I did miss Miami. I did miss my parents, the ocean, and the air. I did miss the food, the music, and the culture. Miami was a lifestyle, and as I got older, I realized why the city got so much praise and attention. It was really paradise, and Miami was always in the back of my heart.

So, yes, I related, too much if anything, but leaving was something I had to do, and I did it for myself and no one else. I needed it. It helped me in ways I never thought it would. In a lot of ways, leaving saved me, but—and there is always a "but"—from time to time that same exact question would appear.

I wonder if he misses me. The thought would suddenly come to me and it would usually arrive when I was home, alone, lying on my bed, wondering if he, too, was thinking the same thing at the same time. Wondering if he was missing me, thinking of me, and remembering what we once had. Many nights I stayed awake, and many nights I contemplated about Owen, my Owen. I would think about random things like the first year we spent together and the last as well. Some nights I couldn't rest, and during those sleepless nights I had all these memories of us shuffling within themselves, piling over themselves, one on top of the other, fighting for a chance to be remembered. I struggled with this almost every night. I struggled with the way things ended, but out of all those memories one would recur frequently, and it was the first time he told me he loved me.

It was the peak of summer and I had just turned fifteen. I remember this summer because I was experiencing new things, new feelings, and discovering myself each day. As a young woman, I was letting go of my childhood and welcoming adulthood. I felt good most days, knowing that I no longer would be treated a certain way, talked to a certain way, and above all, looked at a certain way. I no longer was going to be seen as a child. In a lot of ways, I was excited to be a so-called adult.

It was a hot day, the day Owen told me. Miami summers were hotter than Chicago summers, and of course, this was something that took time to get accustomed to. As children we spent most of our days in the pool or in the park, but this particular day, we happened to be in South Beach. My mother would take us to the beach from time to time, and every summer we made frequent trips a habit. It was Harper, Owen, and me.

We were sitting on a bench near the showers. We had just finished our time in the water, and Harper and I had spent the entire day lying on the sand tanning. The day was hotter than usual and our faces felt tight and dry, and my back was stinging because I hadn't put enough sunblock on.

Owen had spent the entire day snorkeling on the shoreline. For some reason that summer he had an obsession with seashells. "I'm collecting them because I like them." He would bicker about it each time, because Harper and I thought it was silly of him to spend most of the time collecting them instead of hanging out with us. He would leave the beach with a two-liter soda bottle filled with them.

By the time it was time to leave, the only thing that was in my mind was the long car ride home. For some reason the car ride home was always the most comforting, and to be honest, it didn't matter where you were coming from as long as you were going home. Harper was quiet during our ride home as she looked out the window. I didn't have to talk to her to know what she was thinking. She would romanticize about the outside, about the passing, the trip back home as I did as well. And she always sat near the window to do so. Whether she was on a plane, a car, a train, she always had the seat where she was able to look outside.

"I always sit near the window so I can take a glimpse at the world as I am moving," she told me one time while coming home from the park. "I always try to remember the places I am passing through, so that maybe one day I can come here and say I remember this place from before."

In a way, it was as if she was trying to be in as many places as she could at once. This was probably why she was always quiet during the ride back home, smiling and perhaps even thinking to herself about the world, about how beautiful it was from the window. She was a bird, and deep down inside all she really wanted to do was fly. All she wanted to be was free, and she wanted to cling to the unknown as if her life depended on it.

Owen, on the other hand, didn't pay attention to his surroundings. He was all about the now. He didn't pay much attention to the yesterday or to the idea of tomorrow. For Owen, everything was today, and as he would always say, "There is only today and today is today."

The entire car ride back I was in and out of a conversation with Owen. He had been acting rather strange the entire week, and I was just about fed up with it. Anytime I said something, he would somewhat exaggerate it in a derogatory way. If I mentioned the ocean was beautiful, he would sarcastically try to embarrass me. If I said I liked a movie, he would insult the movie and find ways to prove how stupid and useless it was.

It had been going on for several weeks, and each week he just got worse and worse. But nonetheless, I would let it slip through the crack of my consciousness and ignore it. I tried to justify it by blaming it on puberty. Sometimes puberty changed people for better or for worse. I say this because before, things were different—not to say that he was a completely different person but he had little knacks here and there.

By the time we got to Four Quarters, it was almost 7:00 p.m. Between traffic and getting something to eat, time moved rather quickly. The sun was about to set, and the sky was filled with orange hues. Harper and Owen got their bags and began to walk home.

"Mom, I'll be home soon. I'm going to walk them home," I asked for permission as I squeezed out of the car.

"Don't be home late," she advised as I closed the car door. There was a nice breeze coming in. The night couldn't have been any more perfect. We began to walk toward Harper's apartment. Her home was the farthest away of the three. We walked her up to her doorstep and stood there. Harper then cracked her door open and stepped inside.

"We had a lot of fun today," she said as half her body stood out from the door and the other half was inside her apartment.

"Yeah, we did. I always have a good time with the both of you," I said, using a fruity tone.

Owen was anxiously looking at his watch. "I really have to go, you two. My dad is going to kill me. He said I had to be home by six and it's past seven. I'm going to hear it."

Owen and his older brother, Michael, had been tossing each other in their living room, and the two of them accidentally broke their mother's ceramic statue, one that had been passed down from generation to generation. He was grounded for three weeks, and his father was beginning to ease off a little. I smirked as he hurried us.

"Ha! That's right. Okay, we'll go now. I have to take a shower anyway," I replied as Harper began to poke Owen.

"That's right. You're an asshole—you break all your parents' stuff," Harper added to the pokes in a playful manner.

"All right, we're going to go. Hey, tomorrow same time, right?" I asked out loud.

"Yeah," said Harper.

"Okay, let's go," Owen said as we both grabbed our bags from the floor and began to walk away from Harper's door.

"Hey, guys, one more thing," said Harper from the crack of her door.

"We know: don't forget you!" Owen and I shouted as Harper began to giggle in the background. She stood there waiting at the edge of her door until we were completely gone and there was nothing left to see but the empty lobby from her apartment floor.

On the way toward my apartment, I gathered enough courage to confront Owen. The three of us were always together, and I thought it was the perfect time to bring it up—that is, his random tantrums and obnoxiously ill-mannered behavior.

"Hey, so, what's going on with you lately?" I blurted without thinking about it twice or three times for that matter. It just came out of me, as if I couldn't take it anymore. I wasn't upset or anything of that nature. I just wanted to know what was going on. Maybe there was a backstory to his crude comments, and I felt as if it were my duty to get to the bottom of it.

"What do you mean?" He was surprised, as if he had no clue what I was talking about.

"C'mon, we've been best friends for a few years. I think I know when there's something wrong with you."

"Nothing is wrong with me. I don't know what you're talking about," he bickered. His face had turned pale, and he almost seemed to have lost his words. He was tense and instantly got defensive. I wasn't sure if I had just insulted him. It wasn't my intention to do so. I just knew there was something on his mind. I could tell. It was all over his face and mannerisms. I had no choice but to think there was something bothering him, and it was bad enough to slightly change his behavior, at least toward me.

"I don't know what you're talking about. You're making things up in your head." His tone insisted that I stop. I already knew where this was going. Every so often we would disagree about something—anything, really—and that would set us apart for a few days. Of course, that was part of a healthy friendship, but I hated fighting. I didn't have the stomach for it.

"You've just been acting weird lately. Like, you're not the same person at times. I just thought maybe, well, something was picking at you and you were taking it out on me," I said carefully as we stood right in front of my doorstep.

"I'm just going to go," he said with this look in his eyes. This lost look as if he had lost who he was and he was waiting for the old him to return home. He stood there looking at me as if he were holding back something he wanted to say. His lips puckered and his body almost seemed as if he were pulsating. He seemed anxious or anxious enough for me to think I was right and there was something on his mind.

That night, he didn't say a word. He just took off. I didn't see him for two whole days. I tried calling him, knocking at his door, and every time I did so, I got no answer. He was avoiding me at all cost. This was my problem with the both of them: I always cared too much.

It was 11:00 p.m. on the third night, and that was when I finally heard from Owen. I was lying in my bed about to go to sleep when I suddenly heard a tapping sound coming from my window. It was Owen. He was the only person to do such a thing since I had moved here.

"Open your window," he suggested from the other side. I lifted my window and didn't say a word. I was upset, not because he had completely vanished for two days but because he didn't trust me enough to tell me what was on his mind. I knew there was something eating at him.

"It's just." He paused. I stayed silent, waiting for his apology to surface. "It's just." He cleared his throat twice as he tried to recollect himself. He was standing on the other side of the window, swaying his arms as if he were about to confess to some horrible act.

"I . . ." He paused again, as if he were having second thoughts about being here.

"Are you okay? Do you want to come inside?"

"No, um, no, I'm good here. It's just, I . . ." He paused again. "Wow, this is harder than I expected," he added. He seemed nervous and I had no clue what was going on. He tucked both of his hands inside his back pockets and took in a deep breath. And soon enough he began to talk. He began to open up about what was on his mind, in his heart.

"Wes, I know I've been hard on you lately, and I don't really know why. I just don't know how to act with you anymore," he murmured. For a second I thought I was out of my mind. *Did he really say that?* I thought. I was taken aback and a little stunned. He didn't know how to act with me anymore? I wasn't sure if that was an insult, let alone something I should be frowning over.

"What do you mean? We're friends, Owen."

"I know," he replied.

I went ahead and continued what I had sought to say three nights before. "I know there's something on your mind. I know because I know you, and I could see this slight change in the way you've been lately. You don't have to tell me, I'm not going to force anything out of you, but I need you to know I'm here for you. You're my friend and I care about you. And I don't care that you've been an ass lately. I just want you to know whatever it is you're going through, it will soon pass. Okay?" I looked at him through the window screen. I wanted to ensure that I was his true friend. I wanted him to know that I was always here to protect him, to protect Harper. I valued their friendship, and I knew it was worth more than anything money could buy.

"I'm in love with you," he sputtered. "And maybe it's wrong of me to feel this way about you, but it's what I feel, and I think I'll always love you no matter what." I stood there in shock. The words that flowed out of him moved me toward the back of my wall, or it felt as if they did anyway. It was an out-of-body experience, as if I had left my body in the back of my room and I was watching it from the moon. This sharp vibration tickled the core of my chest, it came in waves, and its pinpoint location was the center of my heart. I wasn't expecting Owen to say something like that, but deep down inside I felt good, I felt whole, I felt like everything that had ever hurt evaporated toward the edge of the sun. And it was funny, too funny, because I, too, had fallen for him many moons ago; I just hadn't mentioned it to anyone because I didn't want anyone to know. It was my secret, my prayer, and my first love. And it came to me so suddenly, but I welcomed it with a smile. And yes, maybe at the time I was too young to know what love was and maybe he was too, but I did know one thing: it felt real, and there was no other way to describe what it was he and I were feeling other than love.

That was the night everything changed. That was the night I learned how sometimes the unexpected becomes more than something you used to wish for, how sometimes childhood friends become more than just childhood friends. And how sometimes strangers become lovers and lovers become strangers all over again. That night I found a piece of myself, and I think he did as well.

5

I suddenly opened my eyes. My head was leaning on the window, and I was covered with a tan-colored fleece blanket. I must have fallen asleep without noticing. Coffee had that effect on me. It would instantly give me this raging energy, then take it all away just as fast as it came. It was odd that I fell asleep during the plane ride. I had never fallen asleep on any plane ride as far as I could remember. My paranoia and anxiety would devour me alive, not to mention the half a million different things running through my mind, like the turbulence causing the plane to tilt over and dive straight into the ground. Either way, I guess I couldn't help it. I guess sleep had finally caught up to me and taken over my body without me having any say.

Maybe today was meant to be more than just a regular day. Maybe today everything would sort itself out, problem after problem, and finally make sense. Today was definitely not like any other day, and I thought this because of all the little coincidences that so happened to find me from the moment I had woken up till now. I just had this feeling, this parallel sensation of something familiar, and to top things off, I was on a plane above the clouds in the crack of day, talking to someone who reminded me of him. That was no coincidence, I thought, and today, out of all days, for the last two years, almost everything I saw, felt, and tasted reminded me of her as well.

If I went to the store, something reminded me of Harper. If I went to work, something reminded me of Owen. If I jumped in a car or went down the street for a walk, something was always there to remind me of both Harper and Owen. And today, as all days, the memories had become more than just still pictures hanging in the back of my heart.

It had been two years, two long, miserable years since I had last seen them, but I could still see their faces as if it were just yesterday. And that's what made everything so much more intense. The fact that destiny, a miracle of some sort, brought us together, to rip us all further apart. As I got older, I realized that maybe this was what life consists of. That maybe life was a long series of giving and taking, a long dream that sometimes would turn into a nightmare.

"Welcome back." Owen's voice penetrated my thoughts. I looked toward him, tilted my head, and smiled. At the moment I didn't have much to say to him, although I was beginning to feel more comfortable with him. I guess the more he opened up, the more I did as well. The more he gave, the more I took and in return gave back. The same way Harper did while we were growing up. Some days it felt as if she wasn't there, and other days she was, and I don't mean this in a physical way, but as she got older, she kept more to herself, as if she wasn't sure who she was anymore. She became a mystery, a puzzle, someone who was, at times, hard to understand. There were days when Owen and I couldn't understand her and her actions.

Some days she would just disappear and not be around. Some days she would become a ghost, and she always carried this nothingness in her eyes, this forsaken space that would always be present in her stare, and it was as if the pain she harbored from her father's abandonment had closed her heart in ways that made her slightly unrecognizable. The older she got, the colder her touch became. She was different, and not in a terrible way, to be exact, but in a way that it was enough for us to notice.

We never brought it up to her. We knew doing so would push her further away like a feather being blown by the wind. We knew her sudden change in behavior was always, always the wrong subject to touch upon.

It was fragile and sacred, but sometimes it did come up. I mean, it was inevitable, and every time it came up, he came up, that is, her father. Her mood would change, and it wasn't like we brought him up. She did; she always brought him up when she felt threatened about anything. We always believed that her father disappearing was the root of it all, of her slow change, and I never understood it, not until I saw it happen to me. Until I suffered the same fate as she did a few years later.

I was sixteen at the time, and finally the school year had ended. I was eagerly waiting for my senior year to begin, and deep down inside I was looking forward to another great summer, which meant longer days and even longer nights, days filled with love, laughter, and fireworks in people's eyes.

I always lost myself throughout the year in the chaos of school, relationships, and so on, but it was in the summer when I would find myself again. When I would catch myself in almost everything I saw. With the sun above me, the wind, the ocean, the people, and all the memories that took my breath away. I always found more than I lost during the summer. I always found peace and tranquility. Summer was my heart, and without it I would have lost my mind from the moment I was born.

Since we'd moved to Miami, every summer had been great because of Harper and Owen. We had so much fun throughout the years. From staying up late on a three-way call to riding our bicycles through the neighborhood avenue. From the times we spent sharing laughs to the moments we spent arguing. After all, it was all for a reason, one that was meant to make our bond even stronger than it had been the night before.

In other words, the last four summers of my life had really made me who I am, but this summer was the game changer, and it reminded me how not all things were meant to be perfect, how not all things are meant to be understood. How some things just are. How people just are, and how their actions and decisions are those things that should never be controlled.

It began on a Wednesday, and I remember it was a Wednesday because every other Wednesday after that one changed my entire perspective forever. Owen, Harper, and I had discovered marijuana, and every Wednesday both of my parents would arrive late from work. They would arrive an hour before midnight, and before they arrived, we would open up the windows, turn the AC on, and light a few joints up. That day, we did what we would always do. We were in my room listening to Incubus and watching music videos on MTV while taking puffs off a white boy joint.

Every time we smoked together, we felt different. We felt as if the world couldn't stop us. We felt as if no one could interrupt what we had. We felt strong, without fear and sadness. We felt as if we had each other's back no matter what. In a lot of ways, I think marijuana came to us at the perfect time, because although we had our little issues, every time we smoked together, it felt real. We were open with one another. We would talk about our earlier days and bond as if we were all eleven years old again. We did this every Wednesday. So to say the least, at least once per week, things felt as if they hadn't changed.

"Why don't we drink instead of smoke? Why can't we try beer or vodka or whiskey? Like, why does it have to be marijuana? We should switch it up, try different things, you know?" Owen insisted. I wasn't sure why we would always smoke marijuana. I guess it was how we had started this little ritual of ours. I mean, this is how it had begun, with marijuana, and I never thought about trying other things and we didn't have access to anything else. I, for one, didn't know which beer to drink or what type of vodka, either. Besides, it was Owen's brother who would get us the marijuana, and it was easy to obtain because of that.

"I kind of like this red wine, but I don't know the name of it," said Harper as she lifted her hand and passed Owen the joint. "My mother has this one specific bottle—she gets it all the time and sometimes I try it. It doesn't taste too strong; it's just right. I've tried those drinks you're talking about, the whiskeys and the vodkas. Sometimes when my mother has company over, she lets me try their stuff. They're good and I'm okay with switching over, just anything but beer. Beer is gross, especially when it's hot. It kind of makes me feel bloated and fat the next day. I don't know. I feel like I'm ranting now. Yeah, beer sucks, I'm just saying, but don't listen to me." She was twirling her hand as she continued. She laughed, and sometimes her laughter was contagious.

"Besides, if we bring a different kind of substance, we might not like it, and then our night might be ruined, and I'm not up for another misplanned night," she added as she took the joint out of my hand and took a puff of it.

I had nothing to say to that. At the time I wasn't really interested in drinking or trying other things. I mean, yes, I was somewhat, but our Wednesdays weren't about getting high or drunk. To me, they were more about getting together and hanging out with both of them. I was more interested in the moment and spending it with my two best friends, but other than that, yes, beer was gross. It was disgusting. The taste would make me cringe, and the few times I'd tried it, I'd had to force myself to, and what fun is that? Imagine taking medicine for fun. Like gross cough syrup—how disgusting.

A loud crack came from the door and keys began to shuffle. I turned down the volume coming from the TV. We quickly killed the joint and hid it underneath the bed. The three of us began to flap my pillows to air out the gentle scent of marijuana. I hushed both Harper and Owen, because I wanted to make sure I didn't hear anyone, and I didn't—not until I heard someone call out my name.

"Wes!" Loud and clear, it was my father.

"Oh shit! I'm going to die. I'm dead, holy shit, holy shit, holy shit!" I quietly yelled as I panicked, looking at both Harper and Owen. "What am I going to do?" I looked at Harper as if she would know what to do. "My breath smells like marijuana. Do I smell like it? Do I?" I fluttered toward Owen in fear. I couldn't relax, I couldn't run, and I had no place to hide. "I'm screwed, I'm dead, it's over!" I whispered loudly as I looked toward Harper and Owen.

"Calm down—you're good. You're overreacting. It doesn't even smell like we were smoking at all," Harper comforted me as she placed her hands on my shoulders. "Get a grip. You're okay, honey. Trust me," she continued.

"Wes, come out here. We have to talk." His voice was coming from the living room.

"What the hell? He said we have to talk? He knows! I should have never listened to you guys. Now I'm screwed!" I whispered. "What do I say?" I asked Harper as my face turned red and my eyes began to water.

"Calm down, breathe, tell him you'll be right out," Harper said, and as she spoke, I thought about changing my top.

"I'll be right out," I yelled as I ran toward my closet for a change of clothes. Maybe I was overreacting, but nothing was worse than getting caught. I remember thinking, *Please, God, let this be anything else but this,* and sadly, it was, but nothing in this world could have prepared me for news like this. Nothing could have eased it down, and sadly, I wish it would have been about smoking marijuana in my room, because like I said, for me, everything was about to be flipped upside down.

After a change of clothes, half a bottle of body splash, and six Tic Tacs, I was ready to go out. I told both Harper and Owen to stay in my room quietly. I came out of my room, and both of my parents were sitting at the dinner table with a handful of papers. My initial thought was that one of them had gotten laid off from work and they were just sitting me down to explain how we were going to get through this together.

I was wrong, really wrong. My mother's face was shot red, her eyes were sore, and she looked as if she had been crying throughout the day. Seeing that made me realize how wrong I was. I was trying to be calm, but deep down inside I was freaking out.

"Come here, dear, come have a seat. There's something we have to tell you," my dad empathized. I tiptoed toward them as if I were walking into some forbidden space. I didn't know what to expect other than bad news. Very few times had they given me bad news, so this was the first time in a long time, and I already knew it was terrible. I sat down, and as I sat down, I felt as if I were weightless. I felt as if none of this was real, and the marijuana in my system wasn't helping the situation at all.

"Dear, this isn't easy for us to say and I know you're not going to understand this, but your mother and I . . ." He paused. He took a look at my mother as she began to sob. Then he frowned and held her hand, and then he cleared his throat. That's when I knew it was serious. That's when I knew this was going to be life-changing news. In this lifetime they say you're allowed to have an infinite number of heartbreaks, and some will even encourage you to have as many as you can, but when it came to things of the soul, it was a different story. What I was about to experience was a soul break, and they say that in this lifetime, you're allowed to have only three. Any more could possibly kill you, could possibly leave you in limbo to be lost forever. This was soul break number one, the first of the three I was allowed to have.

"Your mother and I are getting a divorce. I'm going to move to New York, and she's going to stay here with you. Nothing is going to change other than the living situation. I will still talk to you every day, and I will see you at least once a month," he articulated carefully. My mother didn't speak as he explained. I didn't either. I couldn't. I felt as if the air in my lungs were being forcefully pulled out of my body. At the time, I didn't understand what was going on.

I didn't know the truth, and to be honest, I wasn't sure if I really wanted to know. All I knew was that my father was going to leave, and all I could think of was the unimaginable pain I was bound to crash toward too. It was as if this flaming wall of pain had suddenly appeared before me to collapse all over my body and claim me as its own.

And then, it all came crashing down. Every layer of pain was felt. Every cell in my body began to ache. My head and my heart had finally agreed on something. The two didn't want my father to go. "What?" I began to get hysterical. There were a million thoughts racing though my head, and all of them were moving too fast for me to grasp. I was confused. I didn't know what to say, and I didn't cry because it was deeper than that. I froze. I didn't know what to do.

"Mom? Dad?" I looked at both of them. They were serious. This wasn't a joke. This wasn't a dream or a trip off the marijuana. "Mom? Dad?" I kept on. I was a broken record, a broken person with a broken heart filled with an infinite number of broken songs. "Mom! What is going on?" I yelled. I violently lifted myself from the chair.

I stood there and looked at my mom. And then something happened, something unexpected: this explosion erupted within me. It was menacing but not in a physical way. This was something far worse. I rushed toward my room, blowing rage out of my lungs. I stormed off.

"Let her go. She has to learn how to deal with this on her own," I heard my father's voice cloud the background as I stomped my way toward my door.

I slammed the door shut and as I did, all of my picture frames fell and shattered on the floor.

"What happened?" Both Owen and Harper rushed toward me. I paid no attention to them, and tears began to slip from my eyes as I grabbed my book bag and began to fill it with clothes.

"Wes, what are you doing?" Owen's gentle voice was shaking, sounding frightened by what I was exhibiting.

"Wes?" Harper dragged my name out of her mouth as if I wasn't even there.

I continued. There I was, grabbing whatever I saw and placing it into the bag. I put in pants, shirts, socks, underwear—anything I could fit in there, I did, and rapidly. I didn't care. I didn't care about anything at the moment. I wanted to leave. I wanted to die. I wanted to hide in all unfamiliar places, start over. I was being dramatic, but at the moment, it was the only thing I knew how to do.

"Wes, stop!" Owen demanded as he grabbed my hand. "What are you planning to do? What do you think you're doing?"

I yanked my hand from his grip. I wasn't sure what I was doing. I didn't know where I was going to go, but I did know one thing. I didn't want to be here. I wanted to get away as far as possible from my parents, from the world and everything I knew. Maybe it was the marijuana or the news or maybe I was being crazy, but my soul was broken, and now I was left in the void without anyone to run to and no one to comfort me as I looked for a way out.

"I'm running away," I whispered as I tugged through Owen's body. He was standing in front of me, blocking me as if he didn't want me to go.

"What? You can't do that," he said.

"Watch me," I replied.

"What just happened?" Harper asked. I hesitated to answer as I kept filling my bag.

"Wes, if you're going to run away, then I'm going with you," Owen added.

"I'm going too," Harper declared as she began to help me fill my bag with clothes. I didn't say anything. I was sobbing. I felt as if I was drowning in the ocean, stranded all alone in the middle without a single soul to find me, to bring me back toward the shore.

"We're not going to leave you alone. We're with you, and whatever you want to do, we're going to do it too, whether you like it or not," Harper muttered. They were both determined to go. I could see it in their eyes. Hear it in their voices. They were serious. If I left, then they were soon to follow.

Suddenly, I stopped and turned around and faced them. I fell on my knees with a bag full of clothes next to me. I couldn't pick myself up. My body was too heavy. I felt as if I was sinking into the ground. I felt lost like an orphan with no home to call my own. And then, I let go. I let go as if I had been holding on all my life. I let go as if I had a person behind me to catch me as I fell. I let go and then it all just came out.

It came out of my eyes, my mouth, and my nose. It came out of my heart, my head, and my bones. This profound pain shook itself out of me. It vibrated toward the surface and left me alone to die in my very own puddle of pain. I was hurt. I was broken. I felt all types of feelings combined into one unfamiliar feeling. The fear of having people leave you had touched me, and the reality of it was never a sweet flavor to taste.

"They're getting a divorce." That was all I said, and an hour later we did leave, all three of us. We escaped out of my house through the window. Of course, we didn't really run away. We just drove and drove and drove until the sun came up. That night I realized something: how sometimes your friends are more than just friends; they're family. How sometimes your friends are your saviors. I was saved that night, and I could have easily ended up in a different situation. I could have easily lost everything, but I didn't. I became stronger, and I owed it all to them. The two I couldn't get out of my aching soul. I owed them everything, and sometimes gratitude wasn't enough to show them how much I cared. And since then, I've felt as if I was connected to Harper on another level. I've felt as if we went through the same ordeal to understand one another a little more, and we did. We did become closer, but it was only to push us further apart.

"How long was I out?" My voice was nasal and muted. Whenever I woke up, I sounded like a different person.

"Not too long. Fifteen minutes, maybe even twenty. We were talking about my sister, and I saw you slowly doze off again. I stopped talking the moment your breathing changed. It went from a light breeze to a calm rainstorm, and I didn't want to wake you. You just seemed as if you hadn't slept in days."

"It's my job. It doesn't let me rest too well."

"Your job? What do you do?"

"I'm a schoolteacher. This is my second year teaching, so I haven't fully adapted to the schedule. I mean, I have and I haven't. Sometimes I have to take my work home and it gets hectic, but that's work, you know. I'm just glad I have the next week off," I addressed.

I was teaching middle school. Sure, it wasn't the greatest job, but I had kind of fallen into it. Although my degree was in physiology, teaching was a gig that had presented itself, one I couldn't turn down because I needed the money. All my life, I had wanted to be a counselor for abused women; it was our dream. Harper and I were going to open a clinic in her hometown. It had been our goal since we were sixteen. Sadly, I never finished the program; I left Miami way before I had the chance to enroll. I went to the University of Miami. I had completed a bachelor's degree there while Harper was attending Miami Dade College. Owen didn't have the opportunity to continue his education, but he was smart. He knew things. He got around. He was a developer—self-taught—and that alone made him more valuable than the tech kids at the university. He had experience in the field, and because of that he landed a job in a firm where he would program their software. He made good money, and because of his job he was able to move out a few years before I had even thought about leaving home.

"Schoolteacher, huh? My sister is a schoolteacher—a college professor. What are the odds? She works at Berkeley."

"Whose blanket is this?" I interrupted Owen. I was confused for a second. I had his blanket over me, but I couldn't remember if I had covered myself with it.

"It belongs to the airline, of course. I asked one of the stewardesses for a blanket before. It was getting cold in here, so I figured you'd need one too. That's why you've had it on you all along. Did you just notice?"

"Yeah, and thank you," I whispered. It was very thoughtful of him. Although he didn't have to, he did, and in a lot of ways, that made me smile. It made me feel appreciated, as if someone was there for me, looking out for me, protecting me from all odds. For a second, it brought me back to a time when innocence prevailed and trust was a lot easier to come by. And although it was the smallest of gestures, he had gone out of his way for me, and I appreciated that. I appreciated people who did things for others without expecting anything in return. To me, that, too, was another way to be remembered, another way to start a friendship and another reason to have something to smile about.

And yes, maybe I was being too vulnerable, but at this point none of that mattered, because for the past few years my life had been nothing but a headache, and for the first time I felt a little bit more at ease, I felt welcomed, and I felt feelings I hadn't felt in a very long time.

6

I was three hours into the flight. What I was physically feeling before got worse, and being exhausted didn't help much. I got up to walk around. I had to. Sitting down any longer would have given me a panic attack, and that would have been bad, really bad. I was tense. My limbs felt as if they had jolts of energy in them and I couldn't shake it out. It was as if another version of me was trapped within my body, deep within my bones and muscles, and she wanted out, as if she were too big for the skin that was containing her. I couldn't explain it. I just needed to get off this plane already.

"Excuse me," I mentioned to Owen as I passed over his legs.

"Where to?"

"I just have to get up. I'm too anxious, and my body is beginning to get a little tense."

"Okay, well, I'll be here if you need anything."

"Yeah, okay, thanks," I replied as I continued to walk through the aisle. I made it seem as if I had to use the restroom. The stewardess who had brought me coffee was a few feet ahead of me. She smiled as I paced toward her.

"Hello," she said as her smile got even bigger. I nodded and passed right by her. My side of the plane was quiet, but you could hear whispering and hissing on the other side of it, and it was loud enough to hear from the back of the plane. The ambience was that of a small library, that is, if it were filled with two hundred people.

I continued to walk through. By this time I was near the rear of the plane, and this section had so much turbulence that I began to get vertigo. I entered the restroom and closed the door. I turned on the faucet and splashed water on my face and shook my hands as if I were on fire.

I stretched my arms as high as I could, and then I twisted and turned. I placed my arms low, then high over my head, and I twisted and turned again. I did this about five times as my stomach began to rumble. I ignored it and continued. I wanted to jump. I wanted to do squats. I got this urge to get my blood flowing again and was anxious to do so, but being inside a four-by-four-foot restroom above the clouds didn't help much. I did it anyway. I had to.

When I got back, I felt better. The feeling had been alleviated, as if the anxiety I had been suffering from had never happened. At times, when I was undergoing stress, anxiety, or depression, I would take a stroll outside for a few minutes. I would exercise and wear myself out, and to be honest, most of the time that would pretty much take care of it. Sometimes stepping outside gave me a reset. Sometimes a walk had that kind of power; it was a cure for most things, if not all.

It gave me time, and it gave me the ability to think things through—you know, iron things out. If I was overthinking anything, then a walk outside was a remedy. Not a lot of people knew this. Perhaps if they did, then maybe their lives wouldn't be as complicated as some people made them appear.

I sat back down and placed the covers I was given on the empty seat beside me. I folded them neatly and left them there for the stewardess to grab. I wasn't as cold as I had been an hour earlier. I was feeling better, but I was beginning to feel hungry.

I was so hungry that I was actually beginning to consider the airline food. I was willing to do something I had rarely done in my life, and it wasn't like I didn't like it, because I had tried it before. It was just—I just didn't like the way it looked, the way it smelled, and the entire idea behind it. Like I said, it looked fake, as if it were made out of rubber. I mean, how sanitary could it be? And to add, there wasn't a fully functional kitchen on board, and if there was, then that would be preposterous, let alone a hazard. I didn't trust the food, and thinking about having it in my mouth made me gag.

I know, I know, there I go again being overly dramatic, but still I had my points of view, and I wasn't in the mood to try what they had to offer.

As the plane soared above the clouds, Owen and I kept talking. We talked so long that we eventually touched base on every introductory subject there was. We briefly talked about my past, his past, my future and his. Soon enough the conversation hit a wall. We had run out of things to talk about, and of course, then he brought up that one subject I was avoiding. That one subject I didn't like talking about, the one I kept to myself. The one I never for the life of me exposed.

"Hey, I want to ask you something," Owen mumbled as I leaned against my seat.

"Yes?"

"A little earlier, you said I reminded you of someone. What did you mean by that?"

"I knew you would ask that eventually," I said, and then I answered without hesitation. In a lot of ways, ways that didn't make much sense, I wanted to talk about it. Even if it was for a little while, or maybe it was me and I had completely let my guard down. I mean, after all, this Owen wasn't bad company.

"You remind me of my boyfriend, well, my ex-boyfriend. You even share the same name, which I find to be even more ironic," I replied. I took breath in and continued. "It's almost as if I'm seeing him in you. I know, weird enough, but you have so many similarities with him. It's just a little strange," I said as I smiled gently.

"That's good to hear. How long were you two together?"

"Officially about eight years, but we were 'together' for over ten years."

"Damn, that's a pretty long time, especially for someone young."

"Yeah, but time flies, and when you think about it, eight years might seem like a lot. In fact, to most people an eight-year relationship might feel like a jail sentence, but in all reality, it's not. It's all in the way you look at things, and eight years will walk right by you. In other words, it's like, one minute you're with someone, let's say the love of your life, and then the next minute they're gone and you're like, 'Wow, those eight years really got the best of me, they flew right by me, and now I'm left with nothing but these memories.' Well, I'm exaggerating—you wouldn't say that. I don't know. I feel like I'm babbling. I'm sorry, but that's how I feel about that," I confessed. Saying that little part about my relationship with Owen made me feel a lot better, as if a small fraction of the weight I had been carrying for so long was slightly lifted off my shoulders.

"That's a really long time, though, but I get it. I was with someone for six years, so I know what it's like to be committed."

"Oh yeah? What happened?" I asked as he hid the folding table back toward the side of his seat.

"A lot of things happened." He grunted and then he cleared his throat. "For one, we were engaged, and it was strange, because when we fought, we would call the engagement off and then we would make up, and the engagement was on again. We did this so many times, we practically damned the engagement. There wasn't any respect between us. . . ." he said. The first thing I thought was how he was giving me too much information. Information I didn't really want to know. I mean, yes, I had asked what happened, but I didn't really want to know any details. I guess I had brought this upon myself. Maybe he needed someone to talk to like I did.

"Then why were you together for so long?" I cut him off before he was able to finish. To me, there was no point in being with someone if all you did was fight and make up to fight again. *What a terrible cycle to be in,* I thought. If someone was unhappy or if the relationship wasn't working, then why stay so long? I didn't understand those kinds of people. It was strange to me. It was an awful stigma to get into and perhaps even out of.

"Because I loved her and I wanted to make things work, but somehow it would always fall to pieces—once I thought we were okay. And we were never okay; it was always a constant battle. I watched our relationship bloom and die each night. It was bad, but I loved her. I was always willing to fight for her."

"Yeah, I get it," I said carefully. "Sometimes love will make you do crazy things and it's no questions asked. It's something you just do, and even if you know it's wrong, you do it anyway, and as time passes, you think about it and you still think it was worth it even if it was wrong or if you were wrong. You do it anyway. It makes no sense, but either way, I think love and hope are very close to one another," I said.

"Yes, I think so too," Owen said in return.

"For example, when you love, you hope for the best, and when the worst is happening, you still hope for the best. It's hard to explain, but I get you," I murmured. We were beginning to understand one another. It was as if I saw him clearly with no filter and he was standing before me, seeing all of me in return. Being understood felt good. I craved it, and I think we all do every once in a while. I think being understood and loved and cared about is all people live for, and even when things fall apart, people still need to feel understood, loved, and cared for. It is everything. It's everything everyone needs to survive.

"You know what was weird? How I spent every day with this girl and it just ended. This girl knew everything about me, and one day to the next I was a stranger to her. She didn't know me anymore, and I basically didn't know her either. And back then it hurt when I would see her around because I still felt her but I didn't see her, and I think that's the worst. The aftermath of two people is sometimes worse than the problem itself. Life is funny, though, you know, Wes?" He looked far into the aisle as he looked upward toward the ceiling of the cabin.

"One day you're with someone and then the next day you're left alone. Abandoned, you know?" Owen stuttered a little as the edge of his mouth choked on the last thing he said. You could almost see the pain and suffering he had gone through exfoliating from his skin. His eyes were filled with music, sad melodies that only I could hear, and there was horror within him, one you could tell, and it wasn't something he had to say. It was carried by his words and his smile and his lips. He was broken the same way I was broken, and in a lot of ways, I understood him because it was like that for me with Harper and Owen. For over ten years we were always together the same way he was describing the relationship between himself and his ex-girlfriend. For the past ten years I had seen the same people, done everything with the same people, and in a flash, they were gone. They became one with the wind and left a trail of falling sand for me to hold on to.

"But it's all better now, you know?" Owen said. "I got over it. I forgot her and now I'm good, real good, and recently I've seen her around the places we used to hang out in and it doesn't bother me anymore. We don't talk, but that's okay." As he kept on, I couldn't help but think about how broken people always seem to find one another. It is as if we were meant to cross paths, exchange our experiences, and heal one another with our words and stories, together. I was a firm believer in how sometimes broken people fix other broken people, in how sometimes broken things tend to fix themselves as time goes on, because that's how it works, that's how it is. If you've ever felt broken, either time or someone else who was just as fractured as you were would heal you.

But there was a difference between us, between his narrative and mine. While he mentioned how he had grown to forget her, I, on the other hand, couldn't forget my Owen at all. Owen was in my blood, beating through my heart, oxygenating my cells. He kept me going, he kept me alive, although I hadn't seen him in two years. It was the memories that took his place, and those alone were enough to keep me breathing through the twenty-four hours that filled the day. I guess in a way, some broken people are not as identical as they should be. Some are similar, but none are ever the same.

"How did you get over something like that? Sometimes I want to reach out." I paused. "But I fight it, and then I remember the reason why I left my ex-boyfriend to begin with. It's hard to have your mind go against your heart and vice versa. Some nights are harder than others, too, and it's always at night, alone when I'm in my bed about ready to go to sleep when this unjustifiable urge to reach out to him hits me. It feels like a building collapsed over me. I cannot move or think. I just want it to fall before me, but I fight it, and every night I am becoming weaker. I just feel humiliated."

I had broken my silence, and it was something no one had ever heard. It felt good talking to someone about Owen for the first time. I mean, since I'd moved to Atlanta, it had been hard for me to open up to anyone on that level. It was too personal, I thought, and I didn't want to feel like a burden to someone while talking about my past. It was too much and maybe even annoying, and that was the last thing I wanted to be. At times, it was even too much for me to handle. No one ever wants to listen to other people's sorrows. Hell, with so much going on in other people's lives, no one ever has the time for you and your problems. I mean, those are things you have to solve on your own. Right?

"Well, I can't explain it," Owen said. "I just got over it. You know everyone always wants someone to love or to be loved by, but I believe that love or the idea of love is a state of mind. For instance, you love someone because they stimulate you. They give you something you need or want. They drive all of your senses to some high euphoric place that ultimately doesn't exist except in your head.

But what happens when it all becomes a cycle, a routine, something so obvious it doesn't take you anywhere anymore? That's kind of what happened to me." He chuckled as he began to observe the people in the plane. "She just didn't drive me anymore. I got tired. It became so repetitive, the fighting and all that, that I eventually didn't care anymore."

I looked out the window for a split second.

"And I think, at least for me, once I stopped caring, I literally stopped caring. For example, she began to do things I usually didn't like and it didn't bother me. I didn't care if she went out late with her friends. I think, at the time, I even encouraged it!"

"But why did you really stay with her that long?" I repeated my question because it felt as if something wasn't adding up. It's not that I was too interested in knowing what had happened to him. I asked because maybe it would lead me to my own understanding of what had happened to me or to at least answer one of my hundreds of questions.

"I told you, I loved her. So I tried to make it work; I tried to salvage anything I could. I was desperate for a while. But in the end, it's all the same. No matter how hard you try, if it's meant to end, then it will, and if you're meant to go on, then you will too. I just stopped driving myself crazy over her. I guess I got smart or I guess I fell out of love. Not sure," he added.

"I think you're hiding something," I said in a playful manner as I smiled again. I was trying to be funny, but I guess it wasn't working, because he frowned as soon as I said that.

"Are you mocking me, Wes?" he said as his cheeks began to turn red as if he were embarrassed or slightly annoyed. I could understand that. I mean, here you have a guy spilling his guts out and I'm here telling him how maybe there's more. How arrogant of me.

"No, of course not. I would never."

"Right!" he said exaggeratedly, shook his head, and began to smile. "Well, on second thought, other than what I just said, I also think I was bored. Well, not 'bored' per se, but more like I was used to the situation, and I was also attracted to the hurting. I was so used to breaking up every other day to make up a few days later, and I craved it after a while too. It's hard to explain. It's like if we weren't fighting, then something was off. And I wanted to break up several times before, like officially end things, but when I really thought about parting ways, I thought I would miss her or the fighting, I'm not sure. Sometimes I wonder about her, you know. Sometimes I wonder if she ever thinks of me." He took a second for himself and so did I. Everything he was saying made sense, and in that moment, I, too, began thinking about Owen and wondering if my Owen would ever think of me as well.

"Like those few times that she has seen me, I wonder what's going through her mind in that very moment." He had bunny eared the "in that very moment." I thought it was adorable the way he did so and the way he got into his past in detail.

"I don't think that matters," I said. "I think what matters is what goes through your mind when you see her. Anything other than that is like forcing yourself off the boat—to drown. Does that make sense?" I whispered. I was beginning to enjoy this conversation. Although it was about our past lovers, there was something that clicked, and it brought us even closer. People were like that, though: one common understanding of pain brought them closer together and your pain would usually become their very own and vice versa. And it didn't matter if you came from another country, from another culture, from another religion, or anything like that.

Everyone around the world understood the dealings of the heart. The conflicts it brought and heaviness it dragged as it made its way through the door. Pain, yeah, it was that one universal language that connected us all.

"I'm not sure what to think when I see her. Sometimes I feel nothing, and then sometimes I feel as if I want to run up to her and let her know how much better my life is without her. She always thought I needed her and maybe I did, but when I finally let go, it was for the best. It was a new life for me. I was seeing things with new eyes and taking it all in with a new heart. I think I was free." He was grumbling, but he didn't sound too fussy. He was a guy, a really nice guy who had probably gone through hell and back with a girl, probably even a nice girl.

Sometimes love is just a miscommunication, and sometimes that miscommunication can lead to all sorts of madness, like acting a certain way, a way you don't usually act with another person, other than the one you claim to love. It's strange, but love doesn't make any sense, and maybe it's not supposed to at all.

"So what about you? Did you and your ex-boyfriend ever go through that? Like breaking up to get back together to break up again and again?" he asked as the same stewardess from earlier came by our aisle. She sneaked up on us. We hadn't even noticed she was there.

"Is everything okay here? Can I get you anything?" she asked, and then she smiled and tilted her head as her hair fell onto her shoulder.

"No, I'm okay. Thank you," I said.

"I'm okay too. Thanks." Owen's response darted out right after mine.

"No, we never really had a problem," I said. I hesitated to answer him, but he had told me a lot about his past, and I took that under consideration. "Well, there was this one time, before the time it was really over," I said as I shook my head and looked at my feet. I couldn't forget that one time.

I was ashamed of it because it would have been a mistake, and I know I would have regretted it for the rest of my life. At the time, I was confused. I didn't know what I wanted. I didn't know what I needed. I didn't even know who I was, but I did know one thing. I knew my life was headed toward a wall, and so came another boy named Matthew.

It was our last summer before I began college. Harper and I knew how college was going to make our lives even harder, so we took full advantage of the summer. Most days we went to the beach, and at night the two of us hung out by the pier. Most nights there was a drum circle; it was an event on the sand that took place only at night. The locals would have a bonfire and play the drums till 3:00 a.m. It was a great place to meet people, and the law enforcement wouldn't bother us as long as there was no alcohol or other substances on the beach.

At the peak of summer, one night, Harper and I found ourselves together. We were at the drum circle alone. Owen couldn't make it because he wanted to see his guy friends. He was going through a phase where some nights he would see them more than he would see us; therefore, on this particular night he canceled. At first, I didn't think much of it—in fact, I didn't think of it at all. I knew he needed his own space, his own guy friends to talk to about guy things. There was only so much two women could extend themselves to. In other words, there were things we couldn't understand about him and vice versa, and because of that, I understood his needs. Like I said, I didn't think much of him canceling, not until I got to the beach, and that's when things really got to my head.

I was wearing a backless black shirt, and my long curly brown hair ran down my back. I also wore cut jean shorts and a pair of shell-toe Adidas. Harper was dressed the same way except she had her hair picked up and was wearing this green vintage hooded jacket that ran past her shorts. She was carrying a wool bag and her socks were knee high. I would make fun of her because of them. The socks were so big that they sort of looked like leggings.

The wind was strong that night. There was a cool breeze passing through us at all times. The bonfire was flickering and everyone was sitting around it, enjoying the way the flames danced through the night. There must have been about 150 people there, some familiar and some unknown. It was a good night. Everything felt so surreal and dreamlike, as if we were in another dimension, and maybe we were, because that night something unusual happened, something unexpected, something I knew I should never have done.

The sky was pitch black, and the ocean was roaring toward the shore. There's something peaceful about the sounds the ocean makes. There's something that brings out this kind of calmness while listening to the waves. It's almost hypnotizing. It's like being caught in an inevitable spell. That night the drum guys didn't play till 3:00 a.m. One of them had to go within an hour of playing because of a family emergency. It was 10:38 p.m., and I didn't have to be home till midnight. The entire time, Harper and I were sitting on a white blanket over the sand, talking about our future plans. She spoke about how she and I should open a clinic for abused women. She was enthusiastic about it, and listening to her speaking about it made me enthusiastic as well.

"You know, I'm not sure where I'm going to go for school, but I know I'm going to go." She spoke softly as the wind crashed toward her face and made a mess of her front bangs. "I think when we are both done with college, we should open a business together," she said as my hand kept digging into the sand.

"A business together?" I was mesmerized by the bonfire. There were so many people chatting around it. It was as if everyone was in their own little world, and we were as well.

"Yeah, I think we should open a clinic together," she said. I looked toward the sky with a fistful of dripping sand. I was always interested in what Harper had to say, and starting a business with her didn't sound like a bad idea.

"That sounds great."

"I think we should do something for the community, like open a clinic to help abused women to empower them. It's a dream of mine, and I think I'm going to do it. You should definitely think about it. Imagine that: you and I running a clinic together, helping battered women and giving them their strength back," Harper added as sand slipped through my fingers. She was a very special person, and I think she wanted to help women because her mother was abused by her father or something like that. I didn't know the entire story, but Harper said that's why they had split. Nonetheless, I really admired Harper and her hopefulness. If there was anyone to help her build a community center, then I knew it was me.

"That sounds perfect. I could almost see it now," I said as I smiled at her. The mood was almost perfect. After those rare nights when Harper was acting differently, I think this was exactly what we needed: a night on the sand to relate and share our dreams.

Suddenly a guy interrupted us. He was tall, about six foot two. He was wearing surf shorts and sandals. His shirt was off, and he wore a fitted necklace made of beads. His hair was curly, his arms were heavyset, and his body was solid. He was gorgeous, like a wild dream, and I was instantly attracted to him the moment I saw him.

"Hey, this is going to come off really weird, but I'm just going to say it." He spoke eloquently and clearly, with determination in his gaze. "I think you're really beautiful, and I—" He paused, then spoke again. "I just can't take my eyes off you tonight," he said as his eyes were glued to mine. It was a little intimidating at first and at the time, maybe even a little too much for me, but the more he spoke, the quicker he reeled me in. And then, it was as if fate had stepped through the door, and for a second Owen's face appeared through my consciousness as if his image were meant to remind me that he was here.

"Thank you," I said conservatively. I wasn't the type of girl to flirt around, but I was a sucker for charisma, and I couldn't help it. It arguably brought out this friendly, hidden curiosity in me.

That night Matthew stayed with us. He was even kind enough to take us home. He was driving an old BMW. He said it was his father's and his father had given it to him on his eighteenth birthday, which happened to have been three weeks earlier. During the ride home he mainly spoke to Harper. He talked to her about college and how he wanted to be an engineer. He had his whole life planned out, from where he was going to move to exactly which company he was going to work for. He had a strategy for all his goals. He even broke down how he was going to achieve them, and to be honest, that alone made him much more desirable and interesting.

He went on, and I would occasionally smile at him here and there, but I wasn't fully engaged in their conversation. I was just looking out the window, thinking of Owen and how he was beginning to choose his friends over me, over us. And yes, I knew he needed his time with his friends, but lately it had been too much time, and maybe I hadn't enough in me to even mention it.

I just wanted to be understanding, but nonetheless, sometimes I felt neglected, and what was worse was how this was our last summer together and Owen would always sell out at the very last minute for his friends. I know maybe I was being selfish, but still that didn't make things easier for me; it made them harder, and by the end of the night, like I said, things really got to my head.

When we got to our community, Matthew parked his car and asked me to stay for a second. Harper sensed her cue to leave and she did what any other best friend would have *not* done. She left, and that was something I wasn't expecting at all.

"I'd like to see you again," Matthew said formally.

I didn't know what to say. I wasn't sure if I was already breaking the rules by sitting in this car with him alone. I wasn't sure what would happen if Owen were to suddenly walk by and see me. I felt hurried. I wanted to stay, but I wanted to leave. I had a thousand different feelings running through my mind, like an endless stream filled with okays and no's. I was nervous and anxiously looking through the window. And it's not like I was doing anything wrong.

It was just an instinct of mine. I didn't want to cause any problems, because I knew if Owen saw me or if any other neighbor kid saw me, what was happening at the moment didn't look good. I mean, it was midnight, and here I was sitting in some other guy's car in the middle of the parking lot. I was biting my lip over this. I just had to go.

"Um," I said as I re-collected myself. And then I snapped myself out of it. I mean, there was nothing to be exaggerating about. I was overthinking it, and nothing was really happening here. For all I know, Matthew genuinely wanted to be friends, and yes, maybe I was being a tad naïve, but I gave him my number anyway. I mean, I did have feelings for Owen and I did love him, but for all I knew, he could be with another girl right then and maybe he was using his guy friends as an excuse to go see her. I don't know. Maybe I was overthinking it too much. Either way, there was literally nothing going on here. I was indeed overreacting.

"Yes, here's my number. Call me sometime," I murmured.

"Okay, good night."

"Okay," I said as I stepped out of his car and hurried my way back home. That night I knew I had done something wrong and what was to come of it would be even worse, or so I thought. But still, I went with it anyway, and to be frank, I wasn't 100 percent sure why I had done it to begin with.

Matthew and I began to talk on a daily basis. We formed a bond during the entire month of July. I even went to see the fireworks with him, and that was something I had done with Owen since the first year I'd moved to Miami. We would always go to Bayfront Park and it was always a memorable moment, but that year was different.

That year I was enraged with Owen. I was always upset, and every chance we had to spend time together and talk, it ended in an argument. I hated that. I hated that we weren't getting along, and I think a lot of it had to do with me. I expected too much from him. I wanted him to always be around, and I kept forcing him to stay. I demanded all of his time, and I didn't want to share him with his friends.

That summer something got ahold of me, and to this day I don't know what it was. I went from trying to make it work, by giving him his own space, to this concentration-camp Nazi, wanting to control *everything*. I was jealous. I was full of this subtle rage and I tried really hard to let him go, that is, let him grow on his own with his friends, but I couldn't. I was frustrated, and in a lot of ways, that pushed him further away. That summer, what we had once had become a desert, a quiet, lonely place starving for water.

The entire time I didn't know what I was doing. I was blind, and my insecurities led to some unreasonable decisions. I was in over my head and I didn't realize any of it, not until the day he found out about Matthew. That day left a mark on me, a real crack through my skin, head, and heart, and as the years piled, that crack became a scar and that scar made an impact on my life forever. It was a lesson, and like all valuable lessons, it was taught the hard way.

It was July 25, and I had just gotten off the phone with Harper. The entire time I had been talking about Matthew and Owen. Lately, that had become our conversation. Every night I was a roller coaster filled with emotions, confusion. The entire situation was chaos. I felt bad for what I was doing. I was sneaking around doing things I shouldn't be doing. I was lying to my mother. I was lying to Owen and Matthew as well. No one knew what was going on other than Harper, and every night she tried to soothe me.

The complete situation was beyond me. There were some nights when I thought of Matthew and other nights when I thought of Owen, and between those nights I would always weigh my options. I mean, by no means did I want to hurt anyone. I was in a ditch, and every day it was getting harder for me to breathe, to get out of it.

I liked Matthew, I really did. He was always there for me; it was as if he was waiting for me, waiting for me to call him when I needed him most, and he was always there. For example, when I called, he would always pick up on the second ring. When I needed something, he would bring it to me within twenty minutes or less. He was there when I was feeling down and he was there when I needed someone to talk to. In some aspects, he was almost too perfect to be true.

And then there was Owen. Yes, that summer he was hardly around, yes, that summer he had become somewhat of a stranger, and yes, that summer he was so unrecognizable that it was as if he had become a different person, but I loved him. We had history, I knew him, and he had my heart no matter what. But in an odd way, the more he wasn't around, the more I loved, and I missed him so much that it physically hurt me. It was as if my skin had turned itself out and my nerves were exposed. I felt everything, especially the nights he said he would come see me but never showed his face. It hurt but I got used it, to him and his broken promises, but on July 25 he went with his word. He came and it wasn't a pleasant visit.

I heard a knock coming from my window. Of course, it was Owen; he was the only person to do such a thing. I leaned over and opened it. He was standing before me and didn't even give me a chance to say hello.

"What's this I just heard about?" He was angered by the current news he had just discovered.

"Matthew? Are you out of your mind? How long has this been going on?" he continued. He was enraged. I knew he felt betrayed, and I was ashamed because of it. I couldn't hide my face. I knew all of this was bound to erupt, and I knew the outcome wasn't going to be pretty. The entire situation was a ticking time bomb and not just any time bomb; it was a megaton bomb, and I knew once it detonated, *everything* in its path was about to be flattened to dust.

I didn't say anything. I was at fault, but who could blame me? For weeks I had been chasing him down. For weeks I had been yearning for his touch and his company. If anything, I was the one who felt betrayed. It was me who was a victim here, or so I thought. It wasn't fair, but as usual, nothing ever turned out the way I wanted it to.

"Tell me why. Why, Wes?" I couldn't respond, although I knew why and was surprised that he was surprised about the ordeal too. I mean, what did he expect? He was barely around, and I was human. I had needs. I wasn't his pet. I wasn't someone he could go to whenever he wanted to. I was a woman and I knew my worth. And was it so bad that another man knew that too?

"Owen, don't even—" I was upset now, and I was upset because it had taken him this long to even notice the irregularities.

"No, this is bullshit! Behind my back? After everything we've been through?" he said in a panic. The tips of his hands were shaking. You could tell he was devastated. An eerie silence filled my room. My mother wasn't home and she usually didn't interfere in our problems, but I wished she was home to come in and interrupt. I felt terrible seeing him break down like this. It made it all worse. I saw parts of him I hadn't seen before. Parts of him that made me feel sorry for everything I had caused. If only I'd been able to go back in time, I would probably have erased all of it. It was bad, really bad, and watching him fall apart gave birth to a new me, one that promised herself never to hurt this man again in such a way.

That night I hurt him and I hurt myself, but when it was over, it only made us stronger. It brought us back to where we should have been and revived what we once had into something far more beautiful. We took our childlike innocent love and turned it into more, into a blooming flower, and it felt as if a new flame had been born from our dimming light. After that night, we never took each other for granted, and as our lives became more and more complicated, we learned how to manage.

We made time for one another, and together we grew into a deeper love. Eventually, everything went back to normal and I was grateful to have him back as I once had when I was younger.

7

The following year was smooth. Owen and I barely argued, and Harper seemed a little bit more like her old self. She had really bloomed out of her skin. She stood out, her hair had grown below her waist, her eyebrows were slender and fine, and her character had changed in the most heartfelt way. Even the way she dressed had changed. She always looked eloquent, ladylike. Her makeup was neutral, and she always smelled like the ocean. That year, she was cheerful. It was as if nothing bothered her. It was beautiful seeing her happy, watching her take charge of her life and studies.

She was in full control, and she was serious about starting the clinic we had talked about a year or so earlier. She was passionate about her dream and really wanted to make a difference in the community. I guess in a lot of ways, she really wanted to help and save others. It was a privilege watching her grow out of her mold. She was mesmerizing in all her fire and glory. It was as if she had been reborn during our first year of college, and maybe she was, because in those few months it was as if she had reinvented herself. I admired her because of that. We admired her because of that, Owen and I. She had become a woman, a strong, positive light filled with honor and love and tenderness. I loved her; we loved her.

But there was *always* a different side to her, a side that was inevitable, and that side of her would patiently wait within her to surface every once in a while. It was dark, it was cold, and it wasn't pretty or fashionable or reasonable, for that matter. When it appeared, it demanded all of her attention. It drained the sun out of her. It would take her away and leave her in solitude.

I gave her her space when those days arrived, and learned how to make peace with her suffering the hard way. I didn't like standing on the sidelines while knowing something was affecting her. I was always trying to fix things, fix her problems, Owen's, and my own. I couldn't help it; it was my hidden motherly love. I just wanted to help. I wanted to be there. I wanted her to remember me as well for all the effort I put into our friendship. But I learned, and like I said, I learned the hard way. I learned how some things are not meant to be solved.

How some things just are, no matter how bad they are. I learned how certain kinds of pain must happen, and it doesn't matter if you're a good person, a bad person, or lost in between. Sadness, just like happiness, was always waiting on the other side to greet you, to remind you and make you remember how human you were, how imperfect life was, how imperfect my relationship with Owen was, and how imperfect my love for Harper was as well.

But I learned, and I let her be, as much as I hated it. I let her go during those times, but never far enough. I always kept an eye on her, because, well, that's something friends do. They're always there for one another, no matter how far away they go, no matter how bad things get, and no matter how much they change the person or the entire situation. Sometimes a friend can save a life, and because of that I felt as if I should never wander too far away.

When Harper's gloomy days were present, I let her be. I knew when she was having a bad day, because she would call or text me, or reach out to me in some way on a daily basis. But on those gloomy, dark days, she would disappear from the world and the world would disappear from her as if she and everyone else had slipped through her hands. Sometimes I worried about her, but never did I question her isolation.

I just knew there was something wrong. I didn't know how bad things were, but when she would get over whatever it was that was bothering her, things just picked up right where they had left off. She went back to normal, she went back to being Harper, and I went back to normal, and the world kept spinning at the same rate. For a second, Owen and I thought she was bipolar or suffering from some other kind of mild mental illness, but we would say that to each other in good fun. We didn't mean it, and of course, there was nothing wrong with her other than her slight personality shift when she dug herself into a funk.

Apart from that, during our first year of college she had grown to receive a lot of attention from guys. She would, at times, complain about it because they would never leave her alone. She would say, "They're everywhere and they're always watching me, literally. It feels so uncomfortable. If I'm walking to my car, I can feel their eyes following me. It's actually kind of distasteful and creepy."

She would fuss about it with Owen and me every time we were together. Most women would adore that type of treatment, and for a girl who always wanted to be remembered, it was kind of ironic, but Harper wasn't like most girls. In fact, she was the complete opposite. While everyone was going left, Harper was going right, and there were times when she didn't make much sense, but that's who she was. That's what made her, and I think that's why people were always drawn to her. She just had that kind of energy.

She was predictably unpredictable, and because of that, she attracted all kinds of people. But I could see why she didn't like it. I could understand her and relate to her. I mean, imagine that everywhere you went there was a guy lurking somewhere, following you with his eyes, undressing you and fantasizing about you. How uncomfortable!

That year my father and I really bonded. We would talk every other day, and I would go visit him in New York City at least twice a year. I would go at the beginning of the summer and right before it ended. Each visit lasted about a week. Sometimes, Owen and Harper would go with me because they knew how much I hated flying. They took the liberty of accompanying me.

New York City was a good experience; it always brought us back to the basics. It made us feel like we were all eleven years old again. I don't know why. Maybe it was the air, the sounds of the city, or even the way the sun would rise and set over the tall buildings. I always wanted to move there. Not only to be closer to my father but also because it was always an adventure there. For example, every time I was there, I would discover something new about myself, and at random, too. In a coffee shop I found my smile, in Times Square I found my inspiration, and every time I crossed the Brooklyn Bridge, I felt reborn, like a phoenix on fire soaring over the city. In other words, New York had my heart and it had it from the start. It was my home away from home, and it was memorable every time I stepped off the plane.

I always suggested the idea of all three of us moving to New York once our studies were complete. It was perfect. Owen, Harper, and myself in the Big Apple, us against the world with nothing holding us down. That's how it felt at times. Imagine that: three young adults with ambition and an appetite for change. That was my dream, for all of us to stay close and not have life struggles tear us down or separate us. But of course, it didn't turn out that way. It didn't go as I envisioned. It wasn't even close.

Everything happens for a reason, and why things ended up the way they did was something I, too, wanted an answer for. Of course, I never got one. All I got was a blur, and what was worse was what had happened. It really fucked me up. It really blew my world in and left me in the middle of nowhere, or so it felt. Every night since then, I've asked why. I've asked if it was my fault, and maybe it was. Maybe everything was my fault.

"I have this thing, a theory perhaps," Owen said as I dropped my tray beside me. "It's about my ex and what I would say to her if I had the chance to speak to her."

"Oh God, we are still on this subject?" My eyes rolled back as I gave him a smirk.

"Well, yeah, I barely talk to anyone about this. Besides, you're here and I'm here and why not?"

"Okay, just promise me not to make that face anymore." He kept doing this awful face. I think he did it to make me laugh, but I didn't find it amusing at all. It was obnoxious but in a fun way, a playful way. He would raise both of his eyebrows and sort of freeze. He would do so without moving until I replied. He laughed about it as he continued to make the face.

"Okay, okay, I'll stop."

"Thank God." I was being sarcastic. "Okay, so what's your theory?" I added in a tone as if I were poking fun at him and his so-called "theory."

"Well, I have this theory. If I ran into her—let's say she was on this plane."

"Oh God." Already I didn't like where this was going.

"No wait, hear me out." He was enthusiastic about his "theory," as if he had been planning it for several years, researching it, and was finally mastering it to present to the world. He had this spark, the same spark Harper would have fluttering over her when she spoke of her aspirations. "If she was on board and she was to talk to me, I think—"

"What would you do?"

"I would be really polite to her."

"Well, I think that's what you're supposed to do." I frowned and then I laughed, but it wasn't a full-blown laugh but rather a small, delicate, barely noticeable kind of laugh.

"No, wait, I would do it because I know it would bother her. You know, kill her with kindness."

"Oh, you are quite the insatiable killer, aren't you?" I was a bit chatty. He just brought that side out of me. "I think you miss her or maybe you still love her," I continued. There was no explanation for it. The more Owen opened up, the more I saw what was inside his heart. He loved her—of course he did. Why else would he want to keep talking about his so-called ex with some random girl he'd just met on a plane? It didn't make any sense other than he loved her and perhaps, he, like me, was looking for some kind of justification for why things had fallen apart the way they had.

"I don't think I do."

"I think so."

"I don't."

"Well, I do."

"So, what would you do if the tables were turned? What if she killed you with kindness? Have you thought about that? What if—and I say 'what if' to open up the possibility—let's say right now, she is plotting the same thing? She's waiting for the two of you to come face-to-face," I wondered aloud.

I wasn't sure why I had asked to begin with. It's not like I cared. He had said he didn't love her, but I knew he still did. I knew she would cross his mind every night, and if not every night, then every so often. Maybe that's why I connected so much with Owen. Maybe we were going through the same struggle and in some way fate had brought us here to discover something or even find a few answers. Maybe that's why he felt so familiar from the moment I saw him. And maybe, like me, maybe his ex-girlfriend had left some kind of dent in him. You know, a weight, a burden, something he couldn't get away from. Maybe she had left some kind of flawless touch, a deep wound, one he probably still felt. One he probably thought with all his heart wouldn't heal as other wounds had.

Like I said, it was obvious. Here he was, in front of a girl (me) who probably reminded him of her—the exact same way he reminded me of him. Then another response darted out, and this time the tone had completely changed. Just like that, in an instant it went from cheerful to gloomy, as if Owen had opened the window and all you saw were dark clouds caressing the sky.

"I don't know," he said firmly. "Maybe I do. The world doesn't make much sense without the people you love," he murmured quietly as if he were ashamed to say what he was saying.

I thought about it, resonated with it. It was as if an anvil had fallen into the ocean of my soul. He *was* just like me. He was going through the same ordeal I was, and he was probably running like I was. I didn't know what to say. I sat quietly as I looked around, as if I was searching for my response all over the cabin, and he, too, sat there patiently, as if he were waiting for me to tell him why he was still in love with her. The seconds stretched into longer seconds, and soon enough a minute had passed by. He didn't say much afterward, and neither did I. I guess in a lot of ways, that kind of trouble can leave a person speechless. That kind of hurting can leave your mind and your heart out in the woods without a guide to bring you back where you belong.

"I feel the same way," I said.

"Yeah, I know you do," he replied. What an awkward moment. It was not just the silence. It was as if everything in the plane had shifted, as if everyone in the plane was quiet, listening to our troubles.

"I like you, Wes. You know how you said I reminded you of someone? Well, there's something familiar about you, too." He was empathetic, as if he could see right through me. I felt transparent, like a clear balloon floating through the sky and only he had seen me, had figured me out. He had this coherent way of talking to my spirit without the use of words. His eyes connected with mine, and suddenly I began to cry. I knew where it was coming from, and I also knew it was only a matter of time till it all came out of me.

I knew today was a different day. Everything about today had felt different, from the moment I had woken up till now. It was as if every second of this day was connected to something greater. I felt it in my bones. I looked out the window. My hands covered my eyes, but it was obvious what I was doing. A few tears streamed from my face, and once again the only people who came to my mind were the two of them.

I don't know why things happen the way they do. I don't know whom to blame other than myself, and I don't know why such bad things have to happen the way they do, but I do know one thing. I know that sometimes crying replenishes the soul. I know that sometimes each tear carries a truth, one not even I would understand. Tears just are. They're real, and the reason they come out is real.

"I don't know how things got this bad." I tried to make myself stop. I couldn't control it. Their faces flashed through my consciousness as I continued to sob. Owen didn't say anything, and how could he? I had just put him in deep waters. Anyone in his position right now wouldn't have the right words for me, no matter how connected I might think we are.

"Shit, look at me. I'm a wreck," I began rambling. I was incoherent. I myself didn't know what I was saying or doing. It had been two years since I had last seen them, and every month, every day within those two years rushed toward me at full force. I was pinned back. I didn't know what to do, and when I don't know what to do, I usually cry. At the moment, it was all I could do.

"You're not a wreck," Owen advised. "You've just had it rough."

"Haven't we all?" I said in return as I finally got a grip on myself.

"I think everyone has someone they miss. Someone they want to reach out to and tell they're sorry for everything, you know?" He leaned over toward my shoulder as he whispered. "I think if you're not missing someone, then you're not living your life as you're supposed to." He paused as I looked into his eyes. "And I think if you're missing someone, then the possibility of them missing you back is even greater. What a beautiful thing to miss someone, you know? To love someone and not see them again—it kind of makes you appreciate everything once you've lost everything."

He made sense. For the entire flight on the plane he had been making complete sense. It was as if he was slowly breaking my mind apart, taking my thoughts, and realigning them one by one and in no specific order. He was special, and his understanding of life and love was similar to mine. We were both sad metaphors covered in skin. Walking and talking and breathing through moments that broke us, that nearly killed us, and we were taking it all in day by day. I appreciated this moment, and I knew that if I never saw Owen again, I would remember this flight forever.

By the fourth hour of flight I was completely taken away by Owen. I was fascinated by him, and in so little time, I was already beginning to feel as if I had known him for several years. Some people had that kind of effect, that kind of attraction, and clearly he was one of those people. He was an old soul, and the moment I met him it was as if I was meeting an old friend, one I hadn't seen or heard from in several years. I felt close to him, and there was no difference between knowing him for a few hours and knowing him for a few decades.

Our interaction came without barriers, and like I said before, he had something and it was something a little too familiar. He made this flight not too nerve-wracking. He made me feel comfortable, and once again I was convinced that sometimes you have more in common with a stranger than you do with someone you have known all your life. I was happy for our chance encounter; in fact, I hadn't been this calm in years. I felt at ease, at peace, and I found that to be quite surprising. In other words, I was glad to have bumped into Owen. *It was no coincidence,* I thought to myself, and for the rest of the flight I was grateful. I was grounded and I was beginning to feel like the old me.

8

During the second year of college, Harper, Owen, and I did a lot of domestic traveling. We went to New York, Texas, and California. That year, we decided we were all going to move together once Harper and I finished our studies. We had been together all our lives, and it felt like it was the right thing to do. We were excited about it; the only dilemma we ran into was which state we were going to choose to move to.

Harper wanted California because most of her family was there and it had been a goal of hers to move back ever since she was a little girl. She had originally come from California, and throughout the years she would talk about it every once in a while. She loved everything about the state. She loved the coast and the cool Pacific breeze, the beautiful sunsets, and the bright days on the West Coast. She would say how everything about California was different, from the way people spoke to how they walked and lived. The entire West Coast was a lifestyle and a dream for some.

For me, it was indeed a different place and one I could possibly get used to as well. I mean, the weather, the food, the small businesses, and the people were perfect, but I had my own vision too, and my eyes weren't set on the West Coast but on the East. I wanted us to move to New York City, and I wanted us to live there for several reasons. My main reason was the opportunities. They seemed endless there. New York was the Mecca, the building ground for so many great things. It was the birthplace of so many trends, music, fashion, art—you know, things that shook and changed the world. There was so much culture there and so much history, and every time I visited, it was as if my soul was reprogrammed into seeing the world in a different light.

Everything about New York was inspiring, and every time I was there, I felt this positive energy surrounding me and magnifying all my feelings. I felt every drop of inspiration and motivation with intensity. The magnitude of it all: imagine that, imagine feeling everything for a very long time every time you were in New York. Imagine feeling love, feeling hope, and having the two in your hand. Imagine breathing it all in, feeling the city's breath and sound and heartbeat in unison with your very own.

That's how it made me feel, as if I had what I needed to grow in the palm of my hand, and to be honest, each time I was there, I felt like I could conquer the world. I felt real, being there, alive, and the more I visited, the more grounded I was with my location. I was in love. I was captivated, with no way out. New York had me from the start and had me in such a way that no other place had me. I wanted to change the world, and I knew the city of dreams would be the perfect place to spark that fire.

But apart from that, another reason was that my father also lived there, and like Harper, I wanted to be close to my family, considering the circumstances between him and my mother. Now, I'm not saying they didn't get along, because they did. What I am saying is that things were just different, and not in a terrible way, but in an out-of-place kind of way, in a way that took time to get used to. Besides, I always felt as if my father was more understanding and more supportive of my decisions than my mother. She always used logic and reasoning; she always wanted to control everything. I hated that.

I wanted to be my own person, with my own actions—that is, to decide what was best for me without any interruptions. My father, on the other hand, was more spiritual and more of a "go with your gut" type of guy, which was pretty much what my life had recently become.

I didn't put too much thought into certain things. I just felt them, and when something felt like home, I would always follow its path the same way I followed Owen and Harper. But that is not to say I saw eye to eye with where they wanted to live. Harper wanted California, and Owen had Texas. Yes, that was his pick—well, not his "pick pick," but more like he just chose at random, without any reasoning behind it. Unlike Harper and me, he didn't care where we moved. He just wanted to get out of Florida. He, like the two of us, wanted to start a new life, but nonetheless, he had to choose. On the day we decided which state to move to, therefore, he just grabbed a map, taped it on the wall, and threw a dart over his shoulder. It landed on Texas; therefore, he picked Texas.

He said it was fate. He said it was the universe picking the location for us, as if our lives had been prewritten and we were following the next chapter through this string. He believed that if we followed this imaginary string, it would guide us to where we were supposed to be. He would say Texas was our destiny, one that had been carved out for us eons before we were born. Harper and I thought he was crazy. There was nothing in Texas, but either way we chose it to include him in our process. We didn't want to make him feel left out. We didn't want to make it seem as if he wasn't a part of our plans, because that would have been another catastrophe. Besides, we all knew Texas wasn't even an option. Harper and I weren't going to move there no matter what.

On the day we chose, we decided to move to New York. Although, the decision could have changed, we stuck with it until further notice. I was ecstatic about it. I knew from the very beginning we were going to move there. It was written in the stars.

That year was another really good year. Aside from where we were going to move, Harper got a new car and a new job, and she was on the dean's list every semester. One could say she was genuinely happy. Most of the time she was cheerful, and hope ran through her eyes like wild rivers in search of a way out, to flow. She was focused, more than I had ever witnessed. She had become this ball of flame illuminating the sky. We got closer, more than before. We became like sisters, where she would depend on me and vice versa. She had become everything I expected her to be.

I fell into her that year, into our friendship, and I wanted to make sure her dreams came true. I knew she wanted to help women, and I knew from the core of my soul I was bound to help her reach that goal. It had become my personal promise to her. She didn't know it, but I was going to do everything in my power to make sure she got what she wanted. In other words, I was going to be her pillar and support her no matter what.

That year, she also met someone. She had fallen in love with a classmate of hers named Parker. He was a biology major. He was half American, half Cuban. He was tall, about six foot two, with light brown hair and a face filled with freckles. His eyes were light brown and he had this natural tan. He was sweet, funny, and quite the character. He always had something to say, and it wasn't obnoxious or annoying or anything in that field. He was a natural charmer and she would light up every time she talked about him. He romanced her. He made love to her mind and stimulated her thoughts. In her dark days, he brought her back to earth and made her happy.

They were good together too; at times, he would finish her sentences, and every time he spoke, fireworks lit up her eyes. She had really fallen into him, and as the weeks progressed, I knew he had captivated her completely.

Owen and I fell in love with him too. We really enjoyed his company and were even happier to see Harper so enthusiastic about life. Love did that to people. It changed them. It made them better in such a way that only the people around you could see. Yes, love was blind, but from an external perspective, it did change Harper, and for a great cause too.

That summer was a memorable summer. Our party of three had welcomed a fourth, and Owen and I had never seen it coming. But of course, it was too good to be true, and like all beautiful things it didn't last long enough. He soon became a memory, a figment of her imagination, and once again Harper found herself in a very familiar place, a very dark place, a place no one should ever cross alone.

Harper really loved Parker, and when he left, it was as if he took whatever was left of her with him, as her father had when we were children. She once again became an empty shell. She was barely a reflection of her former self. And it was a shame how it didn't last. It was a shame to see her laughter walk out of her life. It was a shame witnessing all of it and not knowing how to deal with it. I mean, the way things happen, you know? The way someone's life can instantly turn itself in another direction is mind-boggling.

The year had begun so perfectly, and it ended in such horrible pain. It was a hard time for all of us, and seeing Harper cry day in and day out was really exhausting. It was draining and hurtful to see her in such despair. She was once again broken, and it broke me watching her go through the storm. But she never went through it alone. I was there, and since our fathers had left when we were younger, we were always preparing ourselves for the worst, but no amount of training or practice can ever prepare you for when something bad happens. There is a difference between expecting something and watching it unravel before your eyes.

In other words, no matter how long you wait for something to happen, when it finally does, it comes to you in such a wave that no matter how good a swimmer you are, you will drown. You will eventually turn in and slip away.

It really killed me; nothing is as sad as watching someone you love go through so much pain. It really hurt—it hurt a lot. And it wasn't even me going through it. Still, I felt it as if it were my very own problem. If only I could go back in time, back to that year, because back then, I didn't even have the right words. I didn't know how to handle it. I was just there, accompanying her with my silence. Maybe that's what she needed: someone to be there with a mouthful of words or not. Maybe just being there silent, hearing her silence, made all the difference she needed. Maybe, but still, I wish I could have done more.

The thing is, toward the end of that year, I was going through a lot. I had too many feelings passing through my heart and they would consist of both pleasure and ache. My heart was sad, but it was also very excited, because that year, that one bittersweet year, Owen had finally presented me with a breathtaking ring. It was what dreams were made of. Owen, after all those years, had finally asked me to marry him.

There were two hours left until the plane landed. I wasn't sure if I was relieved to finally get off the plane or excited to set foot in San Francisco. The entire time felt too long, as if my entire adolescence had flashed in front of my eyes. Scene after scene, I felt as if I were watching an old film reel unfolding off the tip of my mind. The entire time I had been thinking about her and him and how it all turned out. Never in my life would I have thought that things would end up the way they did.

That day was a day unlike any other day. The sun was on the tip of the horizon. I was on top of the world. On top of the rain and wind and all of the sadness and happiness that covered the earth. It was moments like those when I should have been grateful to be alive, but I wasn't, and here I was more confused than ever, more confused about my own life and my own decisions. I mean, who was I? I couldn't even answer that. I didn't know who I was. Maybe at one point I did, but that was a long time ago. Considering all the ache I had lived through, any other person would have grown from all those experiences. Any other person would have learned and matured, but I was a rare case. I had become this stone-like treasure chest filled with everything but treasure, filled with fear and regret and lessons I should have learned but didn't.

I was twenty-five years old, and still, I couldn't get anything right. Maybe I had been crazy from the start, since I was been a child, because no matter what I did, whether I stayed or left or tried to make it work, the dots just didn't connect. My life didn't go the way I planned. Maybe that was my lifelong lesson: the fact that there was no lesson at the end of it all and what I had to gain was everything I knew I couldn't have or touch or keep for myself.

Yes, that in itself was a hard concept to grasp, but my God, that was how I felt: like a lost child in a lost place filled with lost people, none of them knowing where to go. None of them had the directions or the drive to find their homes. Imagine that: a world filled with a bunch of lost assholes looking for other assholes to help them find their way. That's how I felt at times. Like an asshole.

Like running in circles wasn't bad enough. My God, how my mood changes so quickly. At times, I wondered what Owen saw in me or what Harper saw in me to have me around for such a long time. My God, what had I become? A monster? Perhaps that was a question with no answer, and maybe it didn't deserve one at all.

"You're awfully quiet," Owen said as the plane trembled slightly. I was looking out the window again. Somehow, I had spent half of this entire flight ignoring the world, looking out the window, and the other half opening up to Owen about my past, not to mention dwelling in it as well. There were moments when I was so drawn by his conversation that I would forget about my own problems, and other moments when I would dwell in them. In between I would feel sorry for myself. I caught myself doing that often. I wasn't sure why. I also caught myself contemplating my past a lot more, especially during this time of year. Besides that, I also caught myself analyzing everything as if I wasn't sure about anything anymore.

The why, what, who, when, and where had become my companions in the search for something I wasn't even sure existed—something I thought would never reveal itself to me.

"I was just thinking," I whispered as a pause filled our space. It was brief but long enough for Owen to find the right sentiment and for me to find the right reaction.

"Thinking? Of?" he muttered as his voice flowed beneath his breath. I caught every word as his mouth opened up.

"My best friend, Harper." Another pause filled the small distance between us.

"Well, that's sweet. How long have you known her?"

"All my life," I muttered. I was distorted. Maybe it was the plane food I had consumed earlier. Or maybe it was the exhaustion; there was only so much I could physically take.

"I never really had a best friend."

"Never?" I reacted. I thought it was strange. Everyone had that one person to run to when the world was falling apart, that one person who you could trust with your life and your secrets. Both men and women needed that one person, and without them, imagine what our lives would look like. We would probably be dragging our feet through the earth, waiting to die, in search of someone to break us down and understand us.

"No, never, I swear," he said.

"That's awful! I mean, sorry to say, but it really is."

"I know it is, but it's all right."

"Yeah. Harper was like that too," I said as my eyes opened up. "At times, she was so nonchalant about people and places and food and music—I could go on about it."

"She sounds like my type of girl." He grabbed his sports bag next to him and placed it on his lap.

"She was everyone's girl." I laughed as I reminisced about her. "People were attracted to her. She was a natural charmer. Even when she wasn't trying to be, she was charming." I was always so proud to talk about her. Everything about her was worth remembering and sharing with other people.

She was my hero and my inspiration, and every day I thought about her. I loved her; she meant the world to me.

"Well, she's lucky to have a friend like you," he said as I smiled. His flirty tone was beginning to grow on me. I didn't know what to feel, but his smile made me feel the warmth I had been lacking for a few years. For once, it was nice being noticed. It was nice having someone to talk to without any strings attached. It made this plane ride, well, unexpected, and looking into his eyes was like looking through a dark tunnel, gazing at the light on the other side. He gave me hope to love again, to explore the possibility again, and to fall into the truths of my past and accept things for how they had happened.

"So where is she? What does she do?" he asked. I knew this conversation would eventually surface. I had been yearning for it. For the past two years I would completely shut off anyone who brought her up. I always saw it coming, and every time I saw it coming, I would change the subject as if my life depended on it. They say that in this lifetime you're allowed to have an infinite number of heartbreaks. Some will even encourage you to have as many as you can, but when it comes to things of the soul, it's a different story. They would say that in this lifetime, you're allowed to have only three. Any more could possibly kill you. This was soul break number two, and it almost killed me.

A cold chill entered my spine and ran through every pore of my skin. For a second I felt as if my body had fallen off the plane. I felt light-headed. I felt as if gravity didn't exist, as if I were floating away into space. My eyes swelled and the air began to feel heavy. I didn't want to talk about it, but I had to. I knew that if I did, perhaps it could be my first step toward sorting it all out. I slowly opened my mouth, and in an instant I spoke. I whispered, and then the words came out of my body, precise, clear, and sharp like a dagger being jolted into my abdomen.

"She passed away," I said. Terrible anguish ran out of my eyes, but I held it in. I teared up every time I said that to myself. I always wished I were dreaming. I always wished that one day I would wake up from this terrible nightmare. Owen just sat there quietly. I didn't expect him to say much after hearing that. He reacted the same way most people reacted when they heard about death. Most people didn't know what to say, and I wasn't expecting him to say anything either.

Death did that to people. It took everything from everyone—that is, their breath, their sanity, and sometimes even their words.

9

We were in our fourth year of college. Harper and I had been searching through various ads and classifieds for a place to live. My father would mail us the local classifieds weekly. Every Tuesday we got this yellow envelope with his initials stamped over it with red ink on the upper-left corner. There were always five sheets of classifieds and ads folded together neatly. The ads were accompanied by a check. Every week my father would send me a hundred dollars. He had been doing so religiously since the day he and my mother divorced. He would always say, "Save your money. You never know when you're going to need it." Almost every time we spoke on the phone, he would remind me of this.

I did it. I saved almost every check and had been doing it for several years now. In the back of my head, I didn't know what I was saving for; I was just doing it for no particular reason other than my father beating the idea into my head for the past several years. I had accumulated about seventeen thousand dollars. It was a lot of money at the time. I guess, in a lot of ways, saving most of it was a good decision, plus I wasn't a very big spender, and the times I did buy myself something, I usually regretted it. I was almost always like this. When I bought clothes, I was excited about it, but by the time I got home, I wasn't sure if I wanted them anymore. At times, I was indecisive about things— almost everything really. And it wasn't just the things I accumulated over the years. It was literally with everything.

What I said, did, thought, where I went, and so on. I overthought everything, and if I did something or said something, when I was home alone, I would ponder what I had just done or said for hours. I would buy something and regret it later, and I could never take anything back, especially the things I said and did. Once I said or did something, it was written in stone and there was no return receipt to take those types of interactions back. Once the interaction happened, there were no do-overs, no exchanges or returns or anything like that. And might I add how overthinking was the suicide, the icing on the cake, the tipping point of no return.

Like I said, I was almost always like this. I had a handful of regrets and a mind that overthought the possibility of almost everything. And it got worse throughout the years. You would have thought otherwise, but it was true what my father would also say: "Life is one great downfall, and as you fall, you have to appreciate the moment and hang on, because as you get older, sometimes things get darker, things get heavier, and all you have is right now, and that's where the light is."

He was always right, because things did get worse; things did, in fact, change; and it all happened in the blink of an eye or at least it felt as if it did. Nonetheless, a lot happened that year—things I would never have imagined that scared and haunted me forever.

"I'm sorry for your loss," Owen said. He had returned to the conversation after a few seconds of silence. He was quiet about it, but like I said, I understood how death did that to people; therefore, I paid no attention to it. I knew how death took away, how death took away almost everything—on both sides too. That is, even when you heard about it, it took away your soul for a few moments and left you with this coldness all over your body. It left you with this abandonment of words and thoughts and sometimes even feelings.

In other words, death or even hearing the news of a death left a violent silence within you, the kind of silence where all you heard were heartbeats echoing through your frequency. You could almost hear everyone's—the whole entire world's—beating all at once in conjunction with your pain, the heavy pain that presents itself after the loss of someone you love.

"I know what it's like to lose someone too," he said. I didn't say anything. I wasn't even sure why I had told him. I could have said anything. I could have said we weren't friends anymore. I could have said she left the country and I hadn't seen her for the past two years. Out of all the things, I said the truth, and it felt as if I was setting myself up again, as if I were reminding myself of all the things I wanted to forget. She had died. Harper had died.

The one I trusted with everything, the dreams we had envisioned, and the life we had before us was gone, vanished into the nothingness of the world where all lost memories go. And it had been a horrible, horrible reality to live with ever since. Nothing made any sense from there on out, and every day since then, I had been living my life hour by hour, second by second, and none of it ever felt as it had before.

"It happens," I replied. I was trying to be casual, but I was everything but casual. I was a wreck, a mess, and the more days that passed, the harder it was for me to let go, because I simply couldn't. I was still holding on, and I wasn't even sure what I was holding on to, to begin with. Was it the memory of Harper or was it the dream we both shared? I couldn't tell the difference anymore. And like I said before, it wasn't easy for me to open up, although I knew it was, at times, the right thing to do.

"And I think everyone knows what it's like to lose someone," I added quickly, because it was true. Everyone has experienced some type of loss in some shape or form, and if they haven't yet, eventually they will. That's life, that's love. Sometimes you win, and every time you win, you lose—that is, in the long run. If you were with someone all your life, then eventually, one of the two would cease to exist. That's a loss, different from the kind of loss lovers are used to, but nonetheless a loss and one just as difficult to overcome.

I think that's what makes this human experience so special: the fact that we are all meant to die, the fact that we are not meant to live forever. Although we want to believe that the connection between us and the people we love is forever, it's not. People die, love dies, and sometimes understanding the two makes suffering feel as if it's meant to be forever. And ironically enough, I still feel Harper close to me, more than ever, more than before, although she is no longer here. I guess that's hope, that's love, and that's me keeping my promise, the one I made many years ago—the promise I made to never forget her no matter what.

"How did she pass away?" he asked. I looked down for an easy way to explain it, for a subtle way to justify it. It was a delicate subject for me, and I didn't want to break down and cry inside the plane, because these types of things never really heal. It could have happened ten years ago, twenty years ago, or more. When it hurts, it hurts, and when it's brought up, it's as if you are revisiting that first moment you found out. The first moment your soul broke. That was me; I couldn't even talk about it, because when I did, the tears would pile up amongst themselves and cause me to drown in the vastness of my own ocean.

"Tell me. Tell me how your friend died," Owen said. His question weaved through my memory, picking out the scenes that ultimately led Harper toward her doom. They came to me in segments and at random, but it had been like this ever since she passed away. There was no escaping it. It was a weight, and I carried it with me everywhere I went. It broke my heart. It was always the last time I saw her that really got me, because if I had known, I would have saved her life, and perhaps I would have been able to make her stay.

"I'm sorry. If you don't want to—"

"No, it's okay," I replied.

There are days that define your life, certain moments that build it, connect it, and piece it together into what it was meant to stand for, what it was meant to be. And although you might believe that some of those days don't particularly belong to the puzzle, they do. Every moment, every breath, every step and choice you make is worth something. And whether you lead yourself to happiness or complete sorrow is up to you.

It began in November, late November to be exact. I remember this because it was the last time we were going to visit New York for the year. And it was the last real memory I had of her, because that year she suddenly vanished into another person. It was our second night there, and the three of us did what we usually did when we visited New York City. We always did the tourist thing. We figured that by the time we all lived there, we would be so used to everything that eventually we wouldn't appreciate the places the city had to offer.

During the day, we would go to the museums and visit all the popular sites such as the Empire State Building, Times Square, Central Park, and so on. It was always a good time, and at night we would either visit my father or go to a local bar for drinks. We felt alive being there. We felt different, in a good way. I think we were better during our New York days than in our Miami days.

The city did that to us. It brought out our souls, our true selves and colors. It made us smile harder and enjoy each other's company far more than we could ever imagine. Again we had found this gentle happiness. Again we had found the reasons why we had all been friends for so long to begin with. Again Harper had found her smile and I had found my laughter.

We were happy, and every time we were there, we were really, really glad to have one another in our lives. That's why her death came to us as a surprise. I mean, the entire time I thought we were all moving forward, only to discover we were all walking backwards. Her death left me distraught; I couldn't fathom where it all went wrong.

On the last day of our visit, the three of us were ice-skating at Rockefeller Center. We had acquired tickets the first day we got there. My father always had them waiting for us a few weeks before we arrived. This, too, was something we did every trip. Harper didn't like ice-skating.

She would go on and rant about how it was a "couples thing, something only lovers should enjoy." I guess she didn't want to seem like the third wheel. Because of this, she would sit out and watch us as Owen and I skated around the rink. She took pictures, and she would always wave at us from afar, laugh, and smile. But that year, Owen and I had finally persuaded her to skate with us. On that particular day, it took us some time but she finally gave in.

The three of us skated together for about an hour. It was a cold night, and it had been snowing all day. The rink was crowded, and the lights made everything seem surreal, dreamlike, and almost too perfect to ignore. The three of us were padded from head to toe, but still, the weather was a bit defeating.

"See? I knew you'd like it," I said as we all sat near the edge of the entrance where the benches were.

Harper began to laugh as she caught her breath. "Yeah, it wasn't that bad. I actually enjoyed it," she replied as Owen shuffled through his pants looking for God knows what. Soon afterward, one of my favorite songs began to play on the sound system. "Our House" by Crosby, Stills, Nash & Young began to play throughout the plaza. It reminded me of when I was a little girl in Chicago.

"I love this song. It reminds me of when I was young," I said as I looked at the lights behind us.

"I love it too," Harper said. "Growing up, it was part of a *Kidsongs* sing-along collection. It takes me back."

"Shit, I can't find my keys. Shit!" Owen said in panic.

The three of us got up to see if we were sitting on them.

"Maybe you left your keys in the hotel," Harper said.

"No, I had them on me. Shit! I have to find them," he said as he continued to pat down his pants as if the keys were going to magically appear from them.

"Don't panic. We'll help you find them," I said.

"Yeah, relax. We'll find your keys," Harper added.

"No, stay here. I'm going to see if I dropped them on the rink. Maybe someone picked them up and left them in the lost and found." Owen suddenly skated away without saying another word. He was upset, but of course, that would have ruined anyone's night. The song continued to play in the background as Harper and I began to talk.

"I can't believe we're actually moving," she said.

"Me neither. It seems surreal to me," I replied.

"Like, a part of me knew I wasn't going to stay in Miami, but I never actually thought it would happen," Harper said, and she trembled as the vapor from her mouth slowly faded above her.

"I feel the same way."

"You do?"

"Well, yeah. I mean, who would have thought, right? I pictured settling out of Miami when I first moved there; I always thought I would eventually go back to Chicago," I said as I watched Owen searching for his keys. He was weaving through the ice, weaving in and out of the people skating. He then looked at me from afar as he frowned.

"And then I kind of forgot about moving back to Chicago," I said. "I knew I wasn't going to be there. I just knew, you know?" I blew warm breath over my mittens.

"Yeah," Harper said. "I'm really looking forward to it."

"So am I," I replied.

"You know, I'm really proud of you," Harper said quietly as the music continued to play. I didn't say anything, not because I didn't have anything to say but because I knew she knew how much I appreciated what she was saying. She was looking far away, as if she were expecting someone to arrive. She was smiling slightly, and then she squinted, placed her hands on her lap, and continued.

"I guess what I'm trying to say is, I've known you and Owen for a very long time, and I'm really happy for the two of you." She paused for a second as if she were recollecting her thoughts. "I'm just really happy right now—you know, being here and all, sitting next to you, listening to great music, and being in the world's greatest city. It's a blessing for me."

I was overwhelmed. She was right. Despite all the little things that go wrong, we were blessed, and I knew I had a lot to be thankful for. There was no greater place to be, with no greater company than the two of them right then, there, in New York City. I was blessed. I was grateful. I, too, was happy, and these little tingling feelings of joy came shooting straight toward me like a boomerang striking my chest. Every fiber of my being was happy. Every inch of my body felt the sweetness of life, easy and uncomplicated, the way things should be.

"You're going to make me cry," I replied. She was touching on a soft subject, and although we had been together for several years, these kinds of moments rarely came. Maybe it was the city, the cold air, or even what lay ahead. All I knew was that Harper was being genuine. She really did care about Owen and me, about our happiness. She was really proud and so was I, for there was no one else in this world I would have been willing to die for, share these feelings with. She was, after all, my best friend, and without her, my journey, my life, would have been meaningless.

"It's true," Harper said as the snow kept piling over us.

"I know it's true," I replied.

"Do you think he thinks of me?"

"Who?" I asked.

"My father. Do you think he ever thinks of me?" It was indeed a good question, but of course, he had to think of her. I'm sure he had his nights when he was probably alone, lying on his bed, thinking of what had happened to his daughter. I mean, if he didn't, he was a monster.

"I'm sure he does, Harper," I said as she rested her back farther into the bench.

"Hey," said Harper as she looked toward the stars.

"Yeah?"

"Promise me one thing," she said in a low, gentle voice.

"Yeah?"

"Promise never to forget me or this moment." It was then that I should have known something was scattered in her mind, in her heart. The energy between us had shifted, and it was as if she were never going to see me again, as if she were saying good-bye.

"Just don't forget me, despite everything I am and everything I will never be," Harper said as she continued to look toward the sky. "Remember me, love me, and cherish what we have." Every night since that one night her father never showed up, she would say to remember her, but that one night in New York City, at Rockefeller Center, was different. Like I said, it was as if she knew she was going to go away and never return.

That was the last night I saw her. I don't mean that was the last time I physically saw her, but after that, she slowly became someone else, someone I didn't recognize anymore. It was as if her body was hollow and what she had once had within had clocked out. She became more isolated, that is, more so than usual. Days would go by and then weeks and then months. And the times we were together, it was as if no one was there. She also became aggressive. There were times when Owen and I wanted to help her, but she would dismiss us and flood herself in rage. Like the time we both confronted her.

"Why don't you let us help you?" Owen said.

"I don't need your help!" Harper said as she lifted herself from the chair. Owen and I were shocked. She was yelling at the top of her lungs.

"We're worried about you," I said.

"Why can't you two just mind your own fucking business?" she demanded as she slammed her fist on the wall. "Stay away from me!" she grunted, and stormed out of the room. I wanted to chase her, but Owen held me and told me to let her go, that maybe it was a phase and that maybe she needed her own space. He understood how forcing ourselves into her problems was wrong and that eventually, when she was ready, she would open up to us. I did just that, thinking things would get better, but they didn't. Everything just got worse and darker and far more absent.

"What difference does it make?" I said as I looked down the aisle of the plane, then back toward the window again. The sun was shining right through me. I was aggravated a pinch. "She's no longer here, and the way she died doesn't even matter anymore." I jerked back a little. For reasons I couldn't explain, Owen asking me how she died irritated me. I wanted to throw him out of the plane. Squeeze him through the window like a crumpled paper bag. I thought it was rather insensitive to ask a complete stranger how her best friend had died. I mean, you had to be a certain type of person to try to build a conversation off a question like that. It was almost unacceptable, rude, and maybe even unforgivable.

"I'm sorry to have asked. I didn't mean to upset you," Owen said. By now it was hard for me to cover my emotions. I made it clear through my passive gestures that it was a topic that made me uneasy. I tried to calm down.

"I know you didn't, but still," I replied. I guess, in a lot of ways, I still wasn't fully ready to talk about Harper. Although I had opened up a little, it just reminded me that the wound was still fresh. It just really put me in the grave—that is, the way she died—but I knew the more I kept it in, the more it would devour me alive. I held it all in, and it was almost as if all this time I had been waiting for something or someone to free me of this burden, like maybe right now, in this very moment, I was being tested. By whom? Now, that was something I couldn't answer, at least not in this very instance.

Maybe it was Harper watching me, testing me, from the other side. Or maybe it was something else—fate, perhaps—making sure I would transition to my next destination with ease. Either way, I couldn't figure it out, and I wasn't even sure if that was what I wanted. Nonetheless, nothing could have prepared me for the day I got the news.

It was a Tuesday when I got the news. I was on my way home from the university. It was my last semester, and I was taking art history and a few other electives. I had taken my core classes in the beginning, and then I focused on my electives. I did that because I didn't want to go through the narrow, dark tunnel of stress during my senior year. I wanted to be stress-free. Besides, I wanted to focus on other things, such as planning my upcoming fall wedding with Owen and stressing over what style to furnish our apartment with in New York City.

But of course, stress was inevitable. If I wasn't stressing over my part-time winter job as a sales assistant for Sears, I was stressing over my mother, and if I wasn't stressing over my mother, it was Owen, and if it wasn't Owen, it was something else. There was always something to stress about. Stress was the shadow you couldn't outrun. It was as if stress was always there, right behind me, reminding me how my life wasn't meant to be easy. How my life was meant to be filled with obstacles—some worse than others, of course, but nonetheless filled with them to make my life harder than what it seemed.

I was about five minutes away from my house when the phone rang. It was about 9:30 p.m. That night I had stayed in class a little later than usual with a handful of classmates, debating about our final project.

I reached over to the passenger side to grab my phone, to see who it was. It was Owen. It rang three times before I actually picked it up.

"Hey, you, what's up?" I said as I drove down the dark road. "Owen?" He didn't say a word, but I could still hear him on the other end. "Owen? Are you there?" I was beginning to get the feeling that something bad was about to happen. My heart began to pound as the silence coming from the other end arrived to greet me.

"She's dead," he said.

"What? Who? What are you talking about?"

I could hear his quiet whimpering coming toward the surface; it was as if he couldn't get his words together.

"Owen?" I said. I was disoriented for a second. I didn't know what was going on. He was beginning to scare me a little.

"It's Harper." He inhaled deeply and then continued. "She's, she's dead." He repeated it over and over.

That was the worst night of my life. The night the world flipped me on my head. What had been up was now down. At the time, I couldn't describe the feeling that had gone through my body, the moment I realized what was really going on. To this day, I can't explain it, but death is a lot like life. You are born confused, trying to figure it all out, and then something happens to someone you love, and it always happens unexpectedly.

Then you are left with even more confusion, with even more questions and even fewer answers. You get thrown back to the beginning, to the moments in your life when you were most vulnerable. It hurts. Yeah, it hurts like hell. Actually, that's not even how it hurts. It's beyond that, and this unforgiving ache you're left with becomes a part of your life. The never-ending feeling of finding and losing never really leaves your side.

And it almost becomes an obsession, the way you try to figure it all out. You begin to think and wonder how it all happened. How it all went to shit. How the sun was swallowed by the moon and how all your dreams suddenly turned into nightmares. The questions arise, and they do so often. Was it my fault? Should I have done more? Day by day these were the questions I asked myself on an hourly basis. Could I have saved her? Could I have done anything more to make her stay?

Since then, I have felt as if it were my fault. I mean, who else could have helped her, and how did I not even notice it to begin with? I knew she was going through something, but why didn't I pay more attention to it? My life had become a mad cycle of pain and darkness, with no way out.

Like I said, this was a soul break, and the moment Owen told me the news, my soul shattered into a million little pieces projecting in all directions, and my arms were too short to reach out and reclaim them as my own.

10

There was about an hour left before the plane finally landed. Surprisingly, with everything I was reminiscing about, the flight was actually the least of my worries. I had gotten used to the turbulence. I had gotten used to the idea of being 40,000 feet in the air. I had gotten used to the gentleman in front of me who kept banging his seat toward me. It wasn't all that bad, and to be honest, the flight wasn't as terrible as I've made it seem.

I mean, besides the fact that I wasn't feeling like myself, this flight was well worth it. I had tried the airline food, which turned out not to taste as bad as it looked, I had met a guy with the same name as my ex-boyfriend, and for some odd reason I had really connected to him as well. To me, that was a lot to be proud of in five hours.

I had also done a lot of thinking. I'd thought about sleeping as soon as I got off the plane. I'd thought about the flight back, and I'd thought about why I was going to San Francisco to begin with. With so much on my mind, the fear of this plane crashing into Lake Tahoe had turned down a notch. It was all in my head—everything, the good and the bad—and during the entire flight I felt as if I were having a revelation.

Like I mentioned earlier, today out of all days felt different. Today, it was as if a miracle was bound to happen. I felt something different in the air, even all the way up here, like a dense cloud of change forming upon me. I mean, me, of all people, trying airline food? Me, of all people, opening up to a complete stranger about my past, about Harper and Owen? Those were topics I never really shared with anyone to begin with. That wasn't like me at all. There were things I had mentioned today that my parents and others had no clue about. Since the tragic death of Harper, I had built walls around all the things that were precious to me, both old and new. But like I said, today was different. Today the sun was, indeed, a little brighter than any other day or at least from what I could remember.

The older gentleman in front of us was snoring. The crowd within the cabin was minding their own business, and the crew—well, the crew kept doing what they had been doing the entire flight. As for myself, well, I felt warm yet cold, sweet yet bitter, dead yet alive. And between all those feelings, I felt nostalgic.

Every time I closed my eyes, I saw Harper and Owen greeting me as they once did when we were children. I saw Four Quarters and relived memories the three of us had created together. The memories were wild, roaming freely through the banks of my memory, together like a pack of wolves looking for an easy way out. They were the loudest in my thoughts. They were the ones I couldn't ignore, the ones I couldn't outrun.

Just when I thought I was getting over my past, something would remind me of them. Something would always reel me in, back to the depth of what hurt. And it was always something small, something stupid and easy to ignore, like an excerpt of a song or a scene from a movie or just me being me in the middle of the city.

It was as if every time I thought I had it all together, I didn't, because when it was all at ease— that is, my life, my thoughts, and even my heart— something from left field would hit me, like a falling rock landing on the base of my head. When it did, I would revert to the beginning, to where it all started, before the pain and the terrible conclusion of Harper, before I met Owen, and before I moved to Florida.

And then it all slowly played itself out. I saw myself leaving Chicago, moving to Florida, seeing a boy outside, befriending him, then seeing a girl outside, befriending her, and the three of us going through our ups and downs. Our story would always pan out the same exact way it had happened. There was no second chance to change things. She always died in the end, and I, as her best friend, couldn't save her.

Day in and day out, the last image of her dug itself into my heart. Watching her lying in her casket made everything that had ever hurt seem like a walk in the park. And I couldn't forget her, I just couldn't. You see, when I made that promise to Harper, that one naïve promise, I did it without knowing how it would affect my life in the long run. Yes, I did promise to remember her no matter what. Yes, every night since then had been hard to live through. If there was hell on earth, this was it.

It dwelled between the moments of despair, between the tears and the heartaches and all the pain you consume with the tragic loss of another human being. It's one thing to hear about death—

yes, there is no doubt that news like that leaves a hole in people's lives—but it's a totally different experience once it reaches your shores, your relatives, your friends, your relationships. Death, like all things, comes with a consequence, and it was one I didn't know how to overcome.

"I'm sorry about everything you've been through," Owen said. "You know, not a lot of people experience that in their lifetime." He leaned toward me. His hands were crossed over his lap. He had this calm, collected tone as if he, too, had experienced the tragic loss of a loved one.

I shyly smiled, not for his sympathy but because in that moment, he saw me. He saw the real me, naked, vulnerable, hurt, and beaten. I was broken down, so broken that I began to cry. One by one, tears fell out of my eyes as if each droplet had a story to tell, as if each droplet was a memory, a collection of events that linked my entire life together. I cried and I cried quietly as I always did when I thought of her, of him. It was as if I was dying alone in the corner of the earth where no people were allowed, just the stench of death and loneliness.

"I'm sorry," I said, wiping my face with my sleeve. "It's just today—today is one of those days." My sobbing slowed down and I began to pull myself back together.

"I know what you mean. I get that feeling sometimes too, you know." Owen leaned back into his seat, reclined it, and placed both of his hands behind his head. "And it's okay to cry. You don't have to apologize for it." He was staring at the ceiling as the plane shook a little. "I feel the same way. I sometimes think of all the people I used to hang out with. You know, once you stop seeing them, they become strangers. Well, they become people you used to know, and then you're haunted by the memory of them." He paused, stretched his arms, then placed them back behind his head and continued. "And although they are not physically dead, I feel as if they are. They are dead to me, you know? It sucks."

I didn't know what to say. I looked at my watch and then looked at his eyebrows. "That's harsh," I replied. What he was saying kind of made sense but not entirely. You couldn't compare not seeing someone for some time to having someone pass away. It wasn't the same concept, although I did understand what he was saying, because my Owen had become someone I used to know. He had become everything I was afraid of losing, and what was worse, I didn't react the way I always thought I would. I changed, and in the most unexpected of ways. I, too, had become someone else, and I wasn't exactly sure who that person was.

And then there was Harper. She, too, haunted my thoughts, but the difference was, I knew where to find Owen. He was a phone call away, whereas Harper was gone—off to some distant place, or so I wanted to believe. I wanted to believe her spirit was still out there and that maybe one day we would be reunited and that I would have an amazing story to tell her.

"Yeah," I said in a weakened tone as if I were tired of the subject. But I wasn't. I got this spellbinding feeling talking about them, thinking about them, and although it hurt, something in my heart reassured me to keep going.

"So is that why you don't talk to your ex-boyfriend? Is that why you broke up with him?" Owen asked. I wasn't sure if that was exactly why we had gone our separate ways, but I do recall that Harper's death had a lot to do with it. I just couldn't recall exactly how it had happened. It just did, and it felt as if it our separation happened from one night to the next.

An entire week had passed, and I was still in denial that Harper was gone. At the time, I think all of my senses had shut down. I wasn't aware of time. I wasn't aware of my primal instincts, such as eating or drinking. I didn't go outside. I didn't speak to anyone. It was as if I had shut the world off completely. No one ever came to my rescue. No one ever asked me how I was doing. It was as if everyone knew what was going on; thus no one ever brought her up.

Harper's death had become a taboo topic, and soon enough, everyone had sort of forgotten about her. Sure, some of her school friends and acquaintances did offer their condolences to her mother, but that lasted only so long. By the second week or so she had faded into the background. She had become nothing more than a story—one that no one, including myself, understood. It was then that the relationship between Owen and I began to deteriorate.

From time to time I would go to this dark place, a place where no one was allowed in. It was cold, it was empty, and when I was there, I felt as alone as I did in the real world. Harper's death had taken everything away from me. It stripped me down layer by layer and left me raw to the bone. It took all of my joys, all of my laughter, and all of my dreams as well. In other words, it took everything I knew of myself and turned me into a new person— one who was barely functioning, one who didn't see the world as it had once been. I was at a standstill, frozen in time, lost in the seconds, and every moment I spent with Owen made it more difficult. We were falling apart.

We were slowly drifting into the inevitable, and there was nothing either of us could do to save what was left of what we had had. And of course, I didn't want such a thing to happen; it all sort of happened on its own. It unwound itself before our eyes like a spinning top and we just stood there waiting for it to stop, waiting for our fate to come crashing down into our world like a comet on fire destined to set everything into flames.

"Yeah, a lot of things changed when she died," I replied as I placed my hand on my tray table. One of the stewardesses had handed me a coffee. I was just getting started with it.

"When was the last time you spoke?" Owen asked as I took a sip from my steaming cup.

"I can't really remember. It's been that long; it's been a few years."

"Are you happy?"

"I think so. I'm not sure," I said. I wanted to be happy, and I really tried to convince myself I was, but I wasn't. I was just a body, working and going through life as if I was following a set of directions. I was hanging on, alive but barely, living each day as it came and doing all the things I had to do to survive.

"So if you saw him, what would you say?" Owen asked as he leaned toward my left.

I thought about it. It's funny, because for months I knew exactly what to say to him, that is, if I ever had the chance to run into him. I had this prescriptive dialogue, and it was all about how much I hated myself for everything, about how sorry I was, as if self-pity was all I knew.

"I don't really know," I pondered out loud. And I didn't. I couldn't have fetched the speech I had for my Owen if my life depended on it. I couldn't remember the speech, and I couldn't remember the last time we spoke, but there was one thing I did remember, and I remembered it as if it were just yesterday.

I remembered how it ended. I remembered that look in his eyes as I told him what was going to happen. I remembered his face. I remembered the scene, what we were wearing, and what the temperature was outside. I remembered why and what and when it ended. I remembered all the little inconsistencies of that day, everything, literally. I remembered the words we exchanged and how they were told. I remembered how I felt. I remembered how hard it was and how my life changed again after he was gone.

They say a death is meant to bring people closer together, but in our case it tore us further apart. It left us hollow, empty, and overnight we went from being lovers to becoming strangers. It was hard, probably harder than accepting the fact that Harper was gone.

Two months had passed since Harper's death, and within that time I had finally graduated. I had all the reasons to be happy laid out in front of me, but I wasn't. I was far from it. I couldn't even celebrate my graduation. It didn't feel right. I alienated myself from it. At first, Owen dealt with her death in his own way. He was quiet. He was odd. He felt distant. There were times when we were together, trying to make sense of what had happened, of why her death had happened the way it did, and of why none of us had seen it coming. There were times when we were okay, and then there were times when this gloomy silence would sneak up on us. We didn't say much when that happened, but we both clearly understood what we were thinking, feeling, and, above all, hiding within our hearts.

That lasted about a month. Soon afterward, Owen began to behave as he once had. He went back to normal. He followed his routine, and it was as if he had forgotten about Harper. That alone infuriated me. While I was mourning her death, he was out partying and living his life as if nothing had happened. That, too, hurt, watching him bypass everything, watching him find his laughter once again. Or maybe it was just me. I couldn't tell the difference either way. Maybe I was jealous because he got back on track before I did.

We were just coming home from a movie. I hadn't been in the mood, but Owen had talked me into it.

"C'mon, you need to get out!" he shouted. "You can't live your life this way. C'mon, get dressed." He was on my doorstep, trying to persuade me to go. He was persistent, and I knew it came from a good place. He wanted me to feel better. He wanted me to forget, even if it was for a little while. He would say I was headed in the wrong direction and living in the past. Nothing good could come from that, he'd say.

"C'mon, Wes." He was firm about it. I stood behind my door quietly. It was slightly cracked, and I was peeking through. You could tell I had been crying about an hour before he arrived because my eyes were swollen, my nose was red, and the bags beneath my eyes were puffy. I didn't want to go out.

"C'mon, let's go," he continued and continued and continued. There was no end to his nagging. He spent about fifteen minutes telling me to get dressed; I finally gave in. The movie was terrible. I can't remember what it was about. It starred Tom Hanks or Leonardo DiCaprio—one of those two, I wasn't sure. It's not like it was important.

By the time we got home, something inside of me had caught fire and the blaze was getting bigger. I couldn't control it. And then, I let it loose. It was out of my hands, as almost everything was. I was angry, and this was something I had held in for the past few weeks. Yes, my life had changed drastically, but that wasn't all. My plans had changed, and there wasn't anything that could have stopped me from what I wanted to do.

"I can't believe you," I whispered, looking down toward my hands. We were parked in front of my house, and it was almost midnight.

"What are you talking about?" Owen said. I was surprised he hadn't seen this coming. What I was about to experience was a soul break, and as they say, in this lifetime, you're allowed to have only three of those. Any more could possibly kill you, could possibly leave you in limbo, lost forever. This was soul break number three.

"I'm leaving."

"Leaving? What do you mean?" Owen turned the ignition switch, and the engine went off.

"I'm leaving," I repeated. My voice cracked, and my heart was too broken to repeat myself again.

Owen's tone suddenly changed. He went from being playful to serious. He was trying to be calm. He was trying to analyze and understand what I was saying. "Wes?" He looked at me, confused.

"I'm going to Atlanta. I got offered a teaching job there." I couldn't look into his eyes. I felt guilty for not telling him, but I was angry with him for how he had forgotten Harper. It sickened me. It didn't mean I didn't love him anymore—my God, Owen meant the world to me. It was just, well, something inside of me just clicked. I felt connected to this decision in the most unexplainable way.

Yes, I was ruined, but I felt as if I had to go, as if something was waiting for me over there. Maybe even a new life. I felt that if I stayed in Miami, I would steadily sink into a black hole and be swallowed alive there. In other words, everything about this place reminded me of Harper: every spot, every coffeehouse, every bar, every street. Everything brought tears to my eyes. Even being with Owen took me toward her. She was everywhere; it was as if she were communicating with me from the other side, making sure I didn't forget her, making sure I remembered her as I had promised when we were children.

I quickly got out of the car. At the moment, I didn't know what I was physically doing. I just beamed out as I slammed the door. I stood still. I heard his car door slam shut too.

"Do you want to explain what you just said to me?" His voice was shaky.

"There's nothing to explain. I just have to go."

He stood in front of me with both his hands on my shoulders. "Wes?" he whispered as he took a deep breath. "What are you doing? I do not understand." He took a step back and waved his left hand over his hair. "You're leaving to go to Atlanta?" he said with both of his eyebrows lifted in surprise.

"Yes, yes, I am."

"Okay, then, I'll go with you—"

"No." I cut him off before he finished his sentence. My eyes shot toward the ground. I had to be strong. I knew he would try to change my mind. I knew he would try to go with me as well.

"Then what are you saying?" He began to walk toward me. "What? You want to break up?"

Then something climbed out of me. It began in the pit of my soul and worked itself onward, toward the edge of my mouth. It was the truth, and it was seeking the light, for a way out. And it always came out, no matter how deep you buried it. The truth would always rise; it would surface toward the edge of the shore for a breath of fresh air.

"It's this place, it's this air, and it's everyone and everything we know," I said firmly as my heart erupted slowly. "And every day I spend here, I feel—I feel like I am dying. Like I'm suffocating on the bottom of the ocean, and all I am doing is asking for someone to help me, to save me, and no one comes to my aid." I began to sob. I began to break again. I began to hyperventilate.

Owen walked close to me and hugged me. "This is about Harper, isn't it?" he said as he looked me in the eyes.

I didn't say a word. It was about Harper. It was always about Harper. Everything, from our past to our present and our future: it all revolved around her, around each other.

"I just can't deal with this anymore," I continued to sob. The tears rolled off my cheeks and onto my sweater. I couldn't control it. My eyes looked the other way; I couldn't look into Owen's eyes. Everything just hurt.

Owen took a step back and then he looked away from me. He took a deep breath and took another step toward me. "You think I'm not affected by this? You think because our best friend died, that what we have is over? I can't deal with reality either, Wes, and I'm trying to be okay. I'm trying very hard to keep it all together upstairs," he said patiently. "And now you want to leave? And just leave everything behind? Everything we have built together? Just like that? What's gotten into you? We're supposed to get married this year." He said with a completely different tone.

"I can't. I can't do this right now." I began to walk away. "I just want to go home."

"No, we are going to resolve this right now. What? You don't love me?" He rushed in front of me, preventing me from going forward. "Wes, don't you love me?" he said seriously. It wasn't that I didn't love him. As I mentioned before, Owen meant the world to me. If he were a bird, then I would be the wind. He had had my heart since we were children, but this was something I had to do for myself, for me. I mean, all my life I had been worrying about other people, worrying about their well-being, but while I was out saving the world, who was out for me? Who was saving me? No one, no one was, and this was the first step into that reality. No one could save me but myself. I knew I had enough in me to save the whole damn world, but still, I had to fix myself before fixing anyone else.

"I do love you, Owen." I gasped for breath as I spoke. I tried to calm the situation by speaking softly. "I have to go. I'm going to go." No one likes to be the bad guy. No one ever wants to watch another person break. No one wants to hurt another person, especially someone they love. And yes, it was a little irresponsible of me, but I cared about myself, too. I wanted to get better. I felt as if I needed to go, to find myself, to find whatever it was I had lost.

"Then why? If you love me, then why are you leaving me behind?" he asked as he began to sob. Then I began to sob some more. It wasn't easy for me, watching him cry. It was one of the hardest things I've had to go through. "I made a promise to you when we were kids," he said. "Do you remember? I was outside your window."

"Yes, I remember."

"I said I'll always love you no matter what." He wiped his face with both of his hands. "I'll always love you. I'll never stop loving you, Wes. Never!"

That was the last time I saw him. About a week and a half later, I moved to Atlanta. It was a big step for me to do such a thing alone, but as I suspected, things didn't get any better. In fact, things just piled on top of me and got worse.

"I think if I saw Owen, I'd tell him I'm sorry," I said as turbulence entered through the cabin.

"Sorry for?"

"Everything."

"Oh."

"Yeah, it was that bad," I said as I pressed my lips together.

"Do you think you're a bad person because of it?"

"I don't know. Sometimes when I think about it, I feel bad. For example, I just left him, and I was going to leave without even telling him. Imagine being with someone all your life and then they just leave. I guess, in a lot of ways, that's exactly what Harper did to me. She just left me without a chance to say good-bye."

"Yeah," Owen said as the gentleman in front of me stood up. His seat almost hit my forehead.

"Yeah, I know," I replied.

The rest of the flight went smoothly. Owen and I continued to talk about our past. We shared so many things in so little time, some we had even forgotten about. Like the first time I drove a car, and the last time he crashed one. Like the feeling I would get when I swam in the ocean and the feeling he would get when he dove into a lake. We went deeper into ourselves, and the more we exchanged, the more we connected. It was as if we were searching for those little pieces of ourselves we had lost along the way. He was a lot of fun, too. He was extremely funny when he had to be and serious when it was needed. Like I said, I felt good with him. He reminded me of them. He reminded me of a time when things were a lot easier, a time when innocence flourished and friendship could move a thousand mountains a thousand miles away.

He was special like they had been special. He had a lot in him, and as we spoke, I thought maybe what he contained was enough to calm my storm, at least for the moment.

11

A flight attendant spoke from the intercom. "Ladies and gentlemen, as we start our descent, please make sure your seat backs and tray tables are in their full upright position. Please make sure your seat belt is securely fastened and all carry-on items are stowed underneath the seat in front of you or in the overhead bins. We should touch down within the next fifteen to twenty minutes. Thank you, and welcome to San Francisco."

It was finally time to land, which was another thing I hated about flying. I dreaded the descending, the inevitable drop of the plane, the way the plane elevated itself a little higher to land, the sudden drops in altitude, and the unlimited possibility of something else going wrong, such as brake failure, wind shear, or the landing gear locking up. I know, being optimistic wasn't one of my strongest suits, but I had my reasons.

I had had several scares with landings throughout the years and they had all been equally terrifying. Nonetheless, I did as the flight attendant asked. I folded my tray table. I placed the copy of *Vogue* I had been reading beneath my seat and fastened my seat belt. I slid my window curtain open and waited for the plane to land. The plane was full of commotion as the stewardesses patiently combed through the aisles, making sure everyone was securely fastened. Everyone was getting ready to land, and I was eager to do so as well.

"We're finally landing," Owen said as he fastened his seat belt and sat upright.

"Yeah, we finally are. It took forever to get here," I said as I nodded.

"Yeah, it did, but sitting here next to you made all of that better," he replied. He smiled and then I smiled. I think I even blushed a little. I looked away, and then I looked toward him and smiled again. I couldn't help it. I got shy, and I wasn't sure what to expect from him after we got off the plane. I wasn't sure if we were going to exchange phone numbers or e-mail addresses or anything like that.

I wasn't sure if we were even supposed to. I mean, it had been a long time since I had felt this good talking to someone, and maybe he would ask for my information, I thought. Maybe we would even find each other on the outside, somewhere in some city, at random, too. I mean, I was up for it, although I really wasn't the type of woman to do such a thing, especially after meeting on a plane. The entire idea of it seemed foreign to me—that is, exchanging information and seeing what happened next. After all, it had been such a long time since I had done so, and vice versa. The idea of doing it felt unbalanced, maybe even a little forced, but like I said, I wasn't completely against it.

I was pensive for a moment. Would we ever talk again? I thought, *Maybe I should take full control of the situation and ask him for his number myself, or maybe I should let fate decide and see what happens, or maybe I should just do nothing and go on about my day.* Either way, I wasn't sure about anything to begin with. I wasn't even sure he was going to ask. I was ahead of myself. Maybe I did want him to ask, or maybe I didn't. I was contradicting myself. A part of me wanted to see him again, talk to him again, but another part just wanted to take things as they were, two strangers keeping each other company for what it was and nothing else. I wasn't sure. I was indecisive. I was yes and no, although I had enjoyed his company and I, too, thought sitting next to each other had made the flight better.

"Is everything okay here?" asked the same stewardess from earlier. She was leaning toward me while my face was flushed red. I was still blushing and trying to recover from it.

"Yes, everything is good here. Thank you," I replied quickly. The stewardess smiled. Owen nodded, and she stood right back up and placed both her hands on her hips.

"Okay, if you need anything, it has to wait till the plane has landed. We'll be landing within the next fifteen minutes or so," she asserted as looked at her gold watch.

Great: here I was again, stressing over the landing. This was why I hated flying. I was paranoid again. I was anxiously in and out of my zone, overthinking and being overly dramatic. Oh God, how I just wanted to land. And what was worse was how I knew I was going to be in San Francisco for about two days, and already I was thinking about getting aboard another plane to head back home. It never ends, I tell you. My life was a lot like this—that is, I felt like a passenger at all times. I was either leaving or arriving, landing or getting on board. To where? I was never sure. To see whom? I would never have guessed it. I was always coming and going, and from time to time I found myself in a standstill, alone, watching my life passing me by.

"Okay, thank you," I said again to the stewardess as I faded back to reality.

"Bye-bye now." She drifted behind us and continued to attend to the other passengers.

A few moments had passed, and I was looking out the plane when once again I began to feel nostalgic. The departure was one thing, but the arrival was another. Every time I got off a plane, it was as if I had been granted a second chance, a do-over, one with new opportunities, people, food, and music. I could go on. The possibility of anything happening was a beautiful thing, for every time I got off a plane, I felt like someone else, a new person with a new set of different feelings and sentiments.

Of course, they didn't last long enough. A few days in, and all those feelings would vanish into thin air and the entire expectation would drown itself because of my past, because of the stresses life brought. Like my first few months alone in Atlanta. When I had made the decision, I thought I was doing the right thing. I thought I was getting a second chance, one to start over and to just let things be without trying to control everything. I was wrong: the more I tried to forget them, the more everything reminded me of them, because when you're from somewhere else, for some reason, everything reminds you of home.

I had moved to Brookhaven, a neighborhood north of Buckhead, south of Sandy Springs. It wasn't everything I had expected. In fact, moving there wasn't necessarily something I had thought out too well. It was just the circumstances, and, well, I needed to get away. That alone was something I couldn't really wait on, and because of that, I didn't have the time I needed to properly adapt to the change, that is, to adapt to the sudden shift and to the way everything unfolded before my very eyes. I just needed something new, something to distract me from my current surroundings, from my current life and from my past—from everything, really. It was a shame, though, because it all happened in the blink of an eye for me. Everything was so sudden, so fast, that I barely recognized who I was, who I was becoming. I barely knew my own thoughts, my own face, let alone my own heart.

I was going from a big city to a suburban area, and it was my first shot at real life—that is, having my own bills, my own career, and my own home. I felt every feeling I had ever imagined—all of them, except the warm welcoming of a new home. I couldn't adapt. I couldn't find comfort. I couldn't look in the mirror, I was a stranger to myself, and I felt like one within my own skin. I couldn't make friends, and I couldn't connect the pieces for what they were.

Day in and day out, all I knew was that during the day, five days a week, I belonged to a group of students, teaching them grammar-school math. It wasn't the worst job in the world, it just wasn't my first choice, but it was the first out-of-state offer I had received. The pay wasn't too bad, and sometimes when the students left, I would sit around the classroom and contemplate my life. I mean, was this all I had been left with? A desk full of papers to grade, a half-decorated apartment, and a place I wasn't really enthusiastic about to begin with? It all felt a tad underwhelming, as if I had half a life filled with half the intentions and aspirations I had once had.

My father would tell me to move to New York. He suggested it every time we spoke over the phone. He would push the idea into my ear as if it were the cure for my broken heart, for the suffering I had been blessed with. Every time he brought it up, I would quickly change the subject or make it seem as if I had an errand to attend to. I just didn't want to hear it. I knew I was wrong, but I wanted to figure it out on my own. If moving to Atlanta was a curse, then that was something I had to overcome myself. He knew that, and still, I had to hear it.

"You should come to New York, dear. This is where you belong. There's so much of you here," he would say. Maybe he was right. Maybe there was too much of me scattered all around New York City, but there was also so much of them. Every corner reminded me of Harper, and the very breeze carried Owen's name as if I were meant to inhale him. They were everywhere; New York belonged to us, to the three of us, to our dreams and to our future.

And because of that, I just couldn't. The very thought of moving to New York made leaving Miami seem irrelevant. After all, I had left to get away, not to be reminded. I had left to find new things, not to be thrown in a furnace full of memories. Moving to New York would have just made the void even deeper, even emptier, like a deep well filled with nothing but this slow, expanding hollowness it was married to.

If I had moved to New York without Harper, the fate Owen and I shared would still have been the same. I would have left him regardless. It just would have happened in New York and not in Miami. We would have shared the same ordeal no matter what. Besides that, New York would have been suicide, so it was logical not to move there. I would have probably died there, every day, without anyone to rescue me.

For the first few months in Atlanta, I kept to myself a lot. I'm sure the other schoolteachers thought I was crazy. Many times I caught myself trying to be interested in their conversation. I forced myself into their worlds, I really did, but if it didn't have to do with the curriculum, then their chatter would enter one ear and exit through the other. It was as if I was there but I wasn't. My body at times had become a tombstone, one I would visit every time I had the chance to.

I found solace in solitude. I found enough of it to help me get by. During lunchtime I would drive my car toward the back of the school and eat my lunch there in complete solitude. During those moments I minded my own business, played my rock music loud enough, and tried to forget the world. It was my escape. Music did that to me. It was my fix, and at times, it helped. Listening to music became my stress-free safe haven, and it was one I would visit whenever I felt as if I were close to the edge. In other words, whenever I felt down, music brought me back to my senses.

As the weeks progressed in Atlanta, some nights were better than others. Some nights, I didn't need music or anything like that, because I caught myself smiling at things my students had said or done. They always found a way to cheer me up. They always made my life a little better. At times, they gave me the hope I needed to continue, the hope I needed to wake up in the morning and live. And other times, other little things would brighten up my day, little things like walking toward my car and noticing the great weather or being grateful for another day of life.

Because of Harper I thought about death often. I thought about the time she had already missed out on and how things would be if it were the other way around. I thought about her and if she would have missed me as much as I missed her. I thought about her and if she would have found the courage to rise and face the days ahead. I thought about all the things I had been through and how differently she would've reacted. Would she have cried the same tears I cried? Would she have woken up to think of me throughout the day and returned home to think of me again? Would she have wished she had one more night with me, and would she have felt more alone than before?

I also thought about Owen and if he would have done what I had done; that is, if he had been put in my position. I thought about him and if I would have crossed his mind as much as he crossed mine in the middle of the night.

I thought about everything: the hurting, the healing, the forgetting, and the remembering. I couldn't help it. Death did that to me: it made me wonder. It made me obsess over the fact that it could easily have been me. And sometimes it made me feel as if I wanted it to come for me sooner rather than later. At times I, too, wanted to die, but I knew deep down inside that it would have only made everything worse.

It's funny how you're supposed to grow as time goes on. It's funny how you're supposed to learn to forgive yourself and learn to forgive others. For me, it was another story. For me, forgiveness was on the other side of the wall, and it was either too thick to break through or too tall to conquer.

For me, letting go didn't exist, and no matter how much I tried, I always found myself back where it all began. I always found myself back at the root of it all. I always found everything knocking at my doorstep, from the beginning to the end. My story was their story, and anything around it was devoured by the monstrous grin of death, of pain, and solitude.

If anything important happened after Harper's death, it was ignored. It was swallowed and forgotten. Like I said, I had a lot of things to be proud of, but they meant nothing without them. It's not that I didn't make myself available. I mean, new job, new city, new life—that alone would have made anyone else feel as if they had the world in the palm of their hands. It was just me, and what was worse was how I knew that and still did nothing about it. It was me, it was always me, and I didn't want to hear anyone's sympathy.

I didn't want the "you're not alone" crowd to come find me and make me feel a lot more alone than I already did.

I didn't want to be the girl filled with sadness, although I was. Just the idea of being this "freak" made it hard for me to be approachable. I smiled a lot, and almost every day someone would ask me if I was okay. Yes, I was, somewhat on the surface, but within, I wasn't. I wasn't who I had once been, and Atlanta didn't help. I didn't want to leave because I knew if I did, the move wouldn't have meant anything. It didn't represent healing. Anywhere I went, it all felt the same. And besides, what was the point? There was none, in the end. Home was in your heart, and if your heart was broken, then your home was broken, and anything else made everything else feel farther away. It was just a shame I had to go through all of this alone.

"So," Owen inquired. It was as if he were asking me a subtle question—one, perhaps, he didn't know how to ask.

"So," I responded as if I had just asked him the very same question filled with wonder and possibility. Perhaps it was even a question with no answer. I knew where this was going, though. It was beginning to feel familiar. I mean, it was obvious: two people accidentally meeting on a plane, and then accidentally falling into this deep realm of curiosity—to just end it all like that? To go our separate ways and forever wonder "what if?" Like what if I had never gotten on this flight? What if I had missed it? What if I had chosen the plane before or after this one? Would I have met Owen as well? Would I have had a flight filled with so many memories and emotions flowing throughout my stream of consciousness? By all means, he was comforting—young, but great nonetheless—and like I said, I knew he definitely wanted to continue this dialogue beyond the cabin. He probably wanted more. Not to say I didn't—I mean, it was written all over his face. His gestures, his tone, and his entire aura throughout the flight spelled attraction. I knew he wanted more. I knew he was curious to see how it all played out.

There was silence between us. It lasted about two seconds, but for me, to say the least, it was the longest two seconds of the flight. And then, he did what any other man would have done. It was as if he had mustered up enough courage to try to open the door I had kept locked for the past two years.

"So, will I ever hear from you again?" His lips stretched from side to side, and both of his eyebrows lifted toward the ceiling as if he were shy about even asking. He cleared his throat. I smiled, and my smile caught fire. I was excited, but of course, I didn't make it known. Instead, I grunted and made it seem as if he were a burden to me, as if what he had asked was completely out of bounds.

I don't know why I reacted that way, and maybe it was a bit of a surprise for him as well, considering the good company we had shared. I think it was because despite the good conversation, the way he asked didn't feel right. It felt staged, as if we both knew where this was going to end up. I mean, can't two people attracted to one another have a pleasant conversation with it ending right where it began? No, of course not; there must always be more.

Yes, boy meets girl, they have a good time, they exchange numbers, they make plans to meet again, and so on and so forth, and then they eventually fall in love. Isn't that how it usually happens? Then, as with all good things, they begin to take a slow turn. Next thing you know, one of them isn't happy anymore, and that's where the downfall begins: the breaking up we all try to avoid but are all so attracted to, the cycle of running and chasing after one another, that small taste of love.

It's all a scam, this game. No one ever wins, and those who play eventually get burned, and sometimes, at the heart of it all, no one is ever meant to come out of it alive. Love kills, and if it doesn't kill you right away, then eventually it will. Eventually, everyone dies a little every time someone they love says good-bye. Eventually, everything turns to shit, or maybe it's just me and my attitude, the way I see the world. It wasn't the same anymore. Maybe love wasn't any different, but one thing still remained: how you can never outrun love or the awful things it sometimes leaves behind. You can never be close enough to grasp it, and you can never let go when letting go is most needed.

I thought about what Owen asked. I wanted to say yes, but I didn't. Agreeing to it wasn't the first thing I thought of, or the second, or even the third, for that matter. The first thing that I thought about was Owen, my Owen. His face appeared, and because of that, I felt as if I were betraying the man who owned my heart.

"I don't know," I said as I flicked my bangs back toward my ear. His eyes sank within his skull and twitched slightly. It was barely noticeable, but I caught it. I was good at reading body language.

"Oh, well," he stuttered, and then he coughed as he cleared his throat again. He looked toward his side as if he wanted to hide his face, but then he shifted right back toward me. He didn't say anything after that. In fact, we barely spoke; it was as if we had never sat next to one another during the flight. Or maybe, like me, he was waiting for me to say something. Of course, I didn't, and he didn't either. He didn't even look my way, and I didn't look at him, either. Because of that, everything was even more awkward.

It was so uncomfortable that I hardly noticed the landing, and by the time I noticed, we had already touched ground. Despite everything, despite the last six hours I had spent thinking, reminiscing, and conversing with Owen, all we gave each other was a dry good-bye and this strange exchange with our eyes.

It was quiet but also loud enough to say, how sometimes a stranger holds a dagger and can make even the smallest things, like rejection, feel like the end of the world.

12

Almost every time I get off a plane, I find myself waiting over thirty minutes just to get off, but this time the wait was shorter than usual. This time, it took me about ten minutes to get off the plane and wait in the terminal for my belongings. The terminal was full. There were people coming from every direction: upstairs, downstairs, left, and right. The crowd seemed like a dense fog, and nothing was visible other than the continuous stream of bodies walking through the terminal.

So many lives, so many stories and destinations, all moving simultaneously through the walkways. Everyone seemed as if they were in a hurry, everyone but me. I stood there calm like a giant boulder trapped in the middle of a river, and for some reason all I could do was stare at my watch. I kept looking at it, counting the seconds as if I was late, but I wasn't. I wasn't late for anything. No one was expecting me. I was here on my word, on my promise. I was here for her.

It was almost 10:00 a.m. and I was waiting for a cab on the sidewalk right outside San Francisco International Airport. It was gloomy, cloudy, and somewhat cold. A chill ran down my spine as I waited. A slow growling from the pit of my stomach also arose. I felt a sudden, sharp stabbing pain throbbing from the center of my body. I was hungry again, and I felt as if I were being pinned against the wall. I hadn't eaten anything since the third hour of flight; therefore, I knew if I didn't get something to eat now, I would be in a shit mood for the rest of the day. That alone drove me to go back inside the airport to grab a cup of coffee; I knew it would sustain me for at least two hours.

By the time I was back outside, a few minutes had passed. I was happy to be here, and I was happy to know that I had made it here for another holiday season. The more time passed, the harder it was for me to make this trip happen. Every year the weight I was carrying got heavier and heavier. And every time I left this city, I would promise myself not to come back alone.

My father always suggested not going alone. He would always say that if I took someone with me, anyone, the trip would be easier on me than it currently was. He would also always suggest making the trip short. By that he meant no more than one or two days max. I listened to him in that respect. I never stayed for more than two days. I think if I had stayed any longer, it would have made leaving harder every time I came alone.

But I always also thought that if I brought someone, it would only be a distraction from what I came here to do. Plus, if I came here with someone, then perhaps they would want to do the whole tourist thing, and I wasn't really here for those things to begin with. In fact, I never even visited those places from the start. I just wasn't interested.

As I waited for a cab, I looked toward my left and saw Owen standing there. He was a little far from me, standing alone by the other terminal exit. He was smoking a cigarette, and I was more confused than ever. I felt bad about what had just happened, bad enough that I actually walked toward him with the intention to apologize.

"Hey," I said as I tapped him on the shoulder.

"Hey," he said as he exhaled his cigarette smoke. He was surprised, as if he thought we were never meant to cross paths. "I didn't think I would see you again."

"Well, we did just get off a plane," I said, both hands on my luggage. My stare arose from the sidewalk and beamed straight into his eyes. I felt this strange feeling tickling the surface of my skin. I wanted to apologize, but I didn't know how. I didn't want to make it seem as if I were thinking about the way I had neglected him on the plane. My mind was racing. I wasn't nervous; I just didn't want to seem like an even bigger asshole. At least not as big of an asshole as he probably already thought I was.

"I just want to apologize," I said as my eyes fell from his and rolled toward my hands as if my pride had been hurt. He smiled, then chuckled, and smiled again as if he knew I was going to apologize after all.

"It's okay," he replied, but it was a dry reply, not one I came around often.

"It's okay?"

"Yeah, it's okay. I didn't expect anything, to be honest; it was just my gut instinct to ask," he said.

Now I felt like an even bigger asshole. Perhaps it was his gut instinct, and perhaps I had led him to it. I mean, after all, I was being extremely friendly, at least more than I should have been. I felt responsible. Maybe I had led him on a bit. Maybe me opening up the way I had made it seem as if I trusted him, as if maybe I had opened the door for more. And it wasn't that I didn't trust him to begin with; it was just that, like him, my first instinct was not to let him in, at least not here, not now. Besides, he was too young and he was too much like him, and that alone made giving him my number harder. I mean, he reminded me of my ex-boyfriend, for God's sakes, and it would be a little too creepy for me, to be honest.

"It's just, I feel like I owe you an explanation."

"Wes, you really don't. I get it."

"No, I feel like I do." I really did. I really wanted to explain it to him. I wasn't the type of person to lead people on, not that I had done that, but maybe it seemed that way.

"No, you don't," he said. This could have continued for the next hour or so, and maybe I didn't need to explain why I had rejected him, but I did. I just didn't want to leave it like that, because I knew the moment I arrived back in Atlanta, it would be on the tip of my mind. It would have bothered me for who knows how long. I just wanted to tell him why, so I could at least have peace of mind.

"You don't owe anyone anything, Wes. You really don't. No one does," he said again as he finished his last toke and threw his crushed cigarette onto the busy street. He was a little startled, as if my rejection has touched his ego in ways he could not imagine. He did have a point though. In some ways, we don't owe anything to anyone. We are born alone and we are meant to die alone too, no matter who's by our side in life and the moment of death. You're alone and you don't owe anything to anyone in between. On the other hand, you do owe something to the people you love, to those you invest your time in and those who invest their time in you. No matter how long they stay—ten minutes or ten years or even six hours—you owe them gratitude, respect, and appreciation for all the moments they gave you.

That's how I felt toward this Owen. Although I didn't know him, I felt like I did. He had made my flight better, and because of him, I hadn't been too afraid during the flight. He'd made it comfortable, and I wouldn't have changed a thing about it. I would have boarded the plane without hesitation if I'd known he was going to be sitting by my side.

And to be honest, I really took that under consideration. Yes, maybe it had been a bit harsh of me to completely shut him down, which is why I had to say something. I had to apologize or at least give an explanation for why I had reacted the way I had. I just had to do it because I needed to.

"Why don't we exchange e-mail addresses?" I said with a certain kind of glow radiating from my eyes. "I would love to keep in touch with you," I offered as an olive branch. I didn't want to make it seem as if I was suggesting it only out of pity.

Without hesitation he responded and his mood went from dim to bright. "Yeah, that sounds like a good idea."

I smiled as I took out my cell phone and noted down his e-mail address. After that, we stayed talking for a few minutes. He was waiting for his sister to come pick him up, and I agreed to wait with him until she did so. She didn't take long. When she arrived, they both offered to drop me off to where I was going to go. Of course, I declined. I didn't want to make anyone go out of their way for that; besides, my destination wasn't too far away. It was close, about three to four miles out.

We said our good-byes, and by the time I knew it, he was gone and this familiar warmth filled my bones. I was at ease, and once again I found myself smiling at the possibility—the possibility of knowing that somewhere, someone was out there, someone who kind of understood me and saw me for who I was. I wasn't sure if I was ever going to speak to him. It was just good to know I knew where to find him if I ever needed someone to talk to.

"Where to, madam?" the cabdriver asked as I slammed the door shut. The timer was blinking $2.90 in red, and the backseat smelled like wet cigarettes.

"To Woodlawn Memorial Park, please," I said as I adjusted my shirt and fastened my seat belt. It was the first and last thing I did every time I came to San Francisco. Like I mentioned earlier, it had become a ritual of mine. I made sure I came at least two times per year. Last year I'd come more than twice. But those times I would get off a plane and be here for only a few hours, only to turn around and head right back home. I made those random, unplanned trips when I needed them most, when I needed the company.

San Francisco grew on me. It always made sense here. It always felt as if I were home, as if I should have been here from the beginning. Maybe I was looking into it too much, but for some reason, when I was here, I was at peace. I felt like a different person, like someone I used to know. Like my former self.

You know, it's funny how things change. It's funny how you plan your life and it never goes as you envisioned it. No, instead, it goes as you never imagined it would go. For example, you want to go left, but you end up going right. You want to be different, but you end up being the same. You want happiness, but all you get is pain.

Nothing ever goes as planned, and I think that's how it is for everyone. Everyone is mostly content with who they become and never question why they never became more. I mean, here I was, alone in a great city, with no one to share these moments with. I could say life was easier when I was young. Life meant so much more. Everything meant so much more. Yesterday, or the idea of yesterday, was so comforting—that is, my past and everything in it, the good and the bad; both moved me.

Some moments weighed more than others, and other moments really brought me under as if I were going to drown in them, like Harper's loss and my disconnect with Owen, among other things. I guess, in a lot of ways, nothing compared to the amount of pain that brought me. And being here in San Francisco made every bad day in Atlanta worth the wait.

The cab stopped at a red light. The driver leaned toward the passenger-side window, opened it, and threw out his bubble gum. "Here you are," he said in a croaky voice. "Woodlawn Memorial Park, as promised." He flicked his pointer finger on the edge of his timer.

"Eight dollars and sixty-three cents?" I asked as I reached into my bag.

"That's what it says."

"Right. Well, here you go, and thank you," I said as I grabbed my things and closed the door. The exchange was fast. I didn't want to make small talk. I just wanted to do what I had come here for and go about my day. It had taken only nine minutes to arrive, and I was preparing myself for what to expect.

It was surreal, being here once again. Every time I arrived at Woodlawn Memorial, I couldn't control myself. I was always vulnerable here. I always felt as if I were flying, as if I were falling into this deep tunnel filled with sorrow and despair. Every time I was here, before the entrance of Woodlawn Memorial Park, I was reminded of how fragile and delicate life was. And because of that, I felt things, things I wanted to forget but couldn't. I couldn't keep my composure here. I couldn't be who I was before I'd set foot here. I couldn't even pretend everything was okay and I was just another person visiting a beloved one.

Every time I arrived, I came with this expectation, this hope that maybe this had all been a dream, an inside joke, and I would wake up any minute while being here. In other words, I came with nothing, with emptiness and confusion, and I would leave even emptier and even more confused than before.

I walked into the park with a brochure and a visitor sticker on my shirt. I took 78 steps to my left and another 102 steps toward my right. I was surrounded. All around me I had thousands of memories, thousands of goals, and expectations, and dreams, and failures, and lies, and truths. All around me were generations within generations, and together they filled this place with an eerie scent of what had never been and what could have been.

I took a deep glance over to where she rested. She was by a tree, this tree with wide and uneven roots knuckling out of the ground. I had memorized exactly where she was, because I knew she would have done the same for me. I walked toward her, and as I did, I began to feel heavy again; it was as if the sun was tied to one of my ankles and I was dragging its weight with every step I took. I came to a halt. The sky was comforting. It held a shade of gray too beautiful to describe.

She was resting in the back of the park, alone, isolated from everyone else. *She must be lonely here,* I thought. I always thought that. *She must be cold and scared at night. She must be looking for anyone to talk to.* I kneeled and sat down beside her. If only this were all a dream. If only it had been me instead of her. *If only I had known, then perhaps I could have saved her,* I thought.

I sat with a blank face, as if what I was feeling could bring her back. I didn't know what to say or think or do, but I was like this every time I was here. I was always consumed, lost, and weak, but I knew I had to be brave, I knew I had to be strong, because I always felt as if she were watching me. And from the corner of my eyes I always got this feeling, this "you're not alone right now" kind of feeling, this "I'm still with you" kind of thing. I couldn't explain it. I rubbed my hands against the grass, then my hair, and then my eyes.

I sat there quietly for five minutes, looking at the ground as if it was meant to reveal something to me, and then it came over me. A rain, a stinging rain, rough and deep, and it fell from my eyes as if it were meant to cleanse me of my sins. It was as if my soul was leaking out of my pupils. My eyes were like two cyclones carrying my body toward the ground. My cheeks were damp and my face was flaccid. I cried, and I kept crying silently as I sat beside her, above her resting body.

"Hi," I whispered as I sobbed lightly. "It's me again. I'm just here to keep you company for a little while." I gasped for air as the last few tears slid off my chin. It was hard for me to keep myself within balance. Every time I was before her, that is, her grave, I broke down to the very atom. It was something I couldn't avoid. Even the very thought of me being here did the same thing.

Whether I was physically here or in my bedroom, thinking about the last time I had been here, I cried. It was the good-byes that got me. It was how I knew I was never meant to hear her voice again, how I was never meant to greet her and tell her how much I loved her, how much I missed her. It wasn't just leaving that was hard, but arriving, too. Coming to her with open arms was even worse. Saying hello was just as bad as saying good-bye.

"Sometimes I wake up and I forget you're gone. I pick up the phone to see if you've called me." I paused as I collected my thoughts, and then I continued. "Sometimes it feels like you're still here. Like you're watching over me and I'm watching over you." Of course, her death had become a seed, one she had planted right before she died, and it had grown rapidly. It had grown tall enough to leave me beneath this shade, beneath this dark shadowy place I couldn't see myself in.

But apart from that, there was something that was far worse, and it was something I had to take with me to my grave. It was the way she slowly became someone else, the way she slowly walked toward her permanent destination and I did nothing about it. I just watched her unfold into this unrecognizable stranger, and I blamed myself for a lot of reasons. I blamed myself for not doing enough for her, for not stopping her or helping her at all. I blamed myself for the time we were apart and for the long hours she must have felt most alone.

And every night since then I wondered if I could have done more to prevent her tragedy from happening or if I had done enough and it had ultimately led her to her death. I mean, if I had paid a little more attention or put in a little more effort, would she still have been here? And would I have still been with Owen? Would the three of us be somewhere, lost in the city of New York, drinking coffee or listening to music in one of its pubs? I wondered and wondered, and sometimes that was all I did.

I wondered about everything and what had led to this happening. What if we had never met her? Would she still be alive? Would she still be wandering the earth as a stranger? Would she have accomplished all of her goals and become what she wanted to become? These were also questions I was left with. These were the questions I never got an answer to.

"I don't know what to say, Harper," I said. "I don't know what to feel. I miss you, Harper. I miss you every day." More tears rolled out of my eyes. There was no end to their parade. They just kept flowing out of me, and the words I shared with her came out of my mouth without any kind of force.

They didn't need to be pushed out; they simply slipped out and landed on her grave as if they were meant to stay with her. It was hard for me to come, but after all, I had promised to remember her. I had promised to keep her close in my heart, and I had made a promise to myself that since that day her father never showed for her birthday, I would be with her no matter what, for both her birthday and at least one holiday.

"The thing is . . ." I took a deep breath as the sun broke through a cloud and slightly bestowed its shine over me. "Every day I blame myself for not being there for you," I said, kneeling before her tombstone, alone. "Every day I go back and try to make sense of everything. If only I had known then, maybe you could have not slipped away. It's my fault. It's all my—"

"It's not your fault," a deep, unfamiliar voice came fluttering from behind. I firmly wiped my hands across my eyes. I looked back slowly and got up on my feet. I almost tipped over doing so. Before me stood an older man. He was wearing a brown cashmere jacket and a pair of old boot-cut jeans. His hair was trimmed and his face was aged. He was probably in his late fifties, sixties, even. He had a bouquet of flowers in one hand and an ivory envelope in the other. He walked toward her grave and kissed her tombstone. Then he placed the flowers against it. He flicked the envelope, took one look at it, and gently placed it next to the bouquet. He whispered something, but it was so low, I couldn't make anything of it. Then he turned back at me. He reached over with his hand open and spoke.

"Hello, I'm Michael. I'm Harper's father," he said. I, being the overly sensitive woman that I am, almost fainted. I couldn't believe he was standing before me, the man who was possibly the root of all her problems. He was here, beside me, alive and well. It was almost like seeing a myth come to life, a mythological creature walking out of a forest. I just couldn't believe it, and I froze without a thought running through my mind.

13

My mouth became numb. My hands and fingers began to tingle. My body went from cold to warm simultaneously, from hard to soft, from existing to not knowing I was here. Here I was standing before Harper's father, a man I had never met but knew so much about. I had a lot of questions; I wanted to know the same things Harper had wanted to know. Why? Why didn't he claim her? Why didn't he show up that night for her birthday and every night after that? Why did he ignore her? Why did he leave her behind, abandoned like an old record playing the same broken tune over and over? *Why? I mean, why weren't you there? And what did she ever do to you?* I saw her grow up into a beautiful flower only to die for nothing.

For years I watched Harper break a little more as time passed. I watched Harper become a woman, but why, why hadn't he wanted her in his life? That was something the three of us never understood. I mean, as a man, you bring a daughter into the world to just forget about her and go on to live this life as if she had never been conceived? Like I said, even if I'd wanted to, I couldn't align myself with what her father had done.

"Hello. I'm Wes. I'm Harper's best friend," I said using a tone that made it seem as if I wasn't too impressed to meet him, as if I had a chest full of remorse.

"I know who you are," he said.

I crossed my arms and stood there, surprised. "You do? You know who I am?" I said as I tried to recollect the moment we had met. I thought and I thought, but nothing came to mind. I suppose, perhaps, I had met him, but I couldn't remember when it was. I was surprised to not remember him. I mean, Harper's father was a big deal for her growing up, and I would have made the extra effort to remember him. That is, if we had seen him more often.

"I don't recall ever meeting you, sir." I took a step back and squinted as if I were confused. I was confused, for I felt as if I had never met him before. I wondered why he would say he knew me.

"Of course I know who you are. You and Owen were her best friends. You think I don't know anything about my girl?" He took a few steps forward and made a complete stop in front of me. He didn't invade my space; there was enough of it between us to stare at one another's eyes. "I know more than you think," he added.

For a lot of reasons I wasn't spooked by that. It was a bit creepy, but nonetheless, I wasn't affected by it. I wanted to know what he knew, if he knew anything about Harper's death. I wanted to know how he knew about me and Owen as well, considering he had *never* been around.

And then, I just asked. It came out of me without thinking it over. It was a tad rude, but I didn't care. I didn't care about anything. I had had such a hard week that caring about other people's feelings was the last thing on my mind. "How would you know who we are? You were never around to begin with." My voice trembled. My hands and feet did too.

He took a deep breath and looked over his shoulder as if he were ashamed. "I would love to invite you to grab something to eat. Are you hungry, kid? If you want to give me the time of day, I would be more than happy to explain it."

"What do you mean? Now?"

"Yes, now. It's not every day that I get to meet one of Harper's friends. Come on, kid. I'll treat you. I know a quiet little spot by Fisherman's Wharf. There, I'll explain why and how I know who you are, from the beginning." He slowly extended his hand to shake mine.

I didn't agree to it, but the way I nodded, I made it clear that I was open to his offer. Either way, I just wanted to understand. I wanted to give him the benefit of the doubt, for Harper's sake and mine. Maybe he wasn't as bad as he seemed. Maybe there was more to the story, hers and his. All I wanted was some answers, and I didn't care where they came from. I needed something, anything, really, to justify and calm this pain I had rumbling from the bottom of my heart. I felt like a small child in the middle of a hurricane looking for shelter, something to comfort me and steer me away from harm. Anything would have helped. Anything.

"Okay." I agreed, but like I said, I only agreed for the greater good, and I only agreed because he was Harper's father. Sure, one could say, "Hey, this is a complete stranger. Could he even be trusted?" but in a way, he wasn't. In a way, I felt like I knew him, as if we had met many years ago, but it was only because I had heard so many stories during my entire childhood about how wonderful he was, before he vanished. Nevertheless, I didn't feel comfortable, but I did it.

"Okay, great. Let's go," he said as he led the way to his car.

We drove about five minutes. There was barely any traffic, which I thought to be a good thing. We parked near Pier 39, the one by the aquarium, and walked toward a little hole-in-the-wall called Louis'. It was on the second floor, to be exact. There was a hostess by the entrance. She wore a white long-sleeve button-down top with a green bow tie and a little jingle bell hanging from each wrist. Her hair was light brown with small streaks of blond, and it was pulled back in a bun. I took note of it because I was drawn to the way her hair meshed together.

Harper's father was walking in front of me. He hadn't said much in the car, but had listened to jazz and hummed the entire time. Not only did I think it was a bit odd, but I also wondered how this man, this old worn man, could live with himself knowing that his daughter was buried in the ground. I began to sympathize. I couldn't imagine what type of pain he was going through, what type of suffering all of this might have caused him.

But still, I tried not to give him the benefit of the doubt. I tried not to speak to him with an open heart. I mean, after all, he had abandoned my best friend, his own daughter, and for that, no man should ever get off the hook that easily. No man who had done that should be welcomed without a little retaliation. At least not in my eyes.

"Welcome to Louis'. Table for two?" asked the hostess as Harper's father opened the door and held it for me.

"Yeah, it looks like it," he said. I entered the restaurant. It was a quiet, small little place in front of the water. There was no music. No background ambience, just silence. You could almost hear the ticking of the clock as we passed through the front door.

"Okay, right this way," the hostess said as she grabbed two menus and led us toward our table.

We sat down quietly by a window overlooking the water. We didn't say much, perhaps because I didn't have much to say. It was already awkward enough, and I thought how maybe all of this had been a bad idea to begin with. I thought about why I had agreed to this and why I was sitting here with this strange man. I was uncomfortable, and like I said, I didn't have anything to say, and the entire car ride over had been even more out of the ordinary. Everything about this moment felt as if I were getting kidnapped or as if this was a scene from a very bad low-budget horror movie. My eyes were glued to the window as the waitress asked us what we wanted to drink. Outside, the seals were hovering over one another, which was always a pleasant sight for me.

"Do you want to start off with something to drink as you decide what to eat?" said the waitress as she towered over us like a skyscraper aching to fall.

"I'll have a soda. A Dr Pepper, please," I said. My hands were crossed in my lap and both of my feet were dangling from the chair. I was anxious, a bit nervous. I couldn't help it, but I felt as if I was doing something wrong.

"I'll have a coffee for now," Harper's father muttered. He was pensive. Both of his hands were over the table, clenched together as if he were massaging them.

"So where do I start . . ." he said to himself, as if he were thinking out loud. Maybe he was. After all, this had been his idea, and maybe he had enough weight to get off his chest, or maybe he just needed someone to talk to, as we all did.

"So you're Wes," he said as I looked at my fingers. I was like a statue, hard as a rock and closed, like a closet door with a lock. I couldn't look into his eyes. I got this rage when I did. I don't know; I guess I was feeling a lot of different things at the same time. Like I said before, it wasn't easy at first, and making eye contact was something I didn't do. I hesitated to say something, but as the words came out of his mouth, all I could think about was Harper's birthday, the one he missed, the one that had started all of this bitter chaos.

"I'm sorry. I just recognize you from the photos," he said.

The hairs on my arm rose. A light chill ran through my skin. As if this wasn't awkward enough, now he was telling me he'd seen photos of me? *This is all beginning to feel a little too uncomfortable,* I thought. I had to say something.

"From the photos?" Surprisingly, my response came to me like a beam of light guiding me. It was instant, sharp, and precise. I wasn't sure what he was talking about. I wasn't sure what to make of it.

"Yes. Candy, Harper's mother, shows me my girl's things from time to time. Every time I visit, I discover something new about her. It's like I'm rediscovering her, falling in love with her all over again," he said, looking down at the table.

I was confused. To my knowledge he hadn't been in Harper's house for over twelve years or so, and now all of a sudden, he visits from time to time? Since the death of my best friend? It didn't make any sense at first, not to mention, I hated that about people.

People always take other people for granted, especially those they love the most. It was only in the event of a loss that they would take the liberty to finally appreciate what they had. I mean, why hadn't he visited Harper all those years? Why hadn't he been a real father to her? The questions poured out of me faster than I could have ever imagined.

The only one true question that mattered was on the tip of my tongue, the one question any sane person would think of before even giving him a chance to explain himself. I felt like he needed an explanation for his actions or better yet, an explanation for all the things he should have done but hadn't.

"Why weren't you there?" The words catapulted out of my mouth without a thought or a wall to hold them in. He suddenly cleared his throat. Maybe he was going to explain himself, or maybe it was extremely rude of me to ask, but who cared, right? It was the truth. Why wasn't he there? I wanted to know why. I wanted to understand every single bit of it so that I would never fall into that kind of mistake, that kind of carelessness, that kind of reckless behavior.

"Excuse me?" he said. I still couldn't look him in the eyes. I repeated myself, which was something I didn't like to do. "Why didn't you see her? Why weren't you there?" My tone switched. I wasn't sure if I was angry or if I was hurt, hurt for all the things he had caused and hurt for all the things he hadn't caused. My eyes began to swell, but it was only because I didn't know what else to say to him. I wanted to be friendly, I really did.

I wanted to understand him and all the things he had caused, but the other side of me wanted to grab him by his ears and yell, yell everything she had wanted to tell him, both bad and good. I wanted him to feel her pain, know it as if it was his very own, feel it, live with it, carry it, sleep with it, eat with it, walk with it, and try to find love with it as she had tried to do when she was alive.

I was there. I went through all of it with her. I saw all the pain he had caused her. I mean, I witnessed her crying. I felt her every night she felt most alone. I was there. *I was with her.* I was there to comfort her. I was there to brighten her up and lift her back to her feet. Maybe I wasn't the best role model she had or best friend or whatever, but at least I was there. At least I tried, but he didn't even care. He didn't give her the time of day. No visits. No phone calls. No nothing. Just the wait and this broken anticipation, that was all he gave her. What an asshole, to now say it was as if he were falling in love with her again.

He took a deep breath and looked me dead in the eyes. I turned away quickly. "It's a long story, Wes," he said, frowning.

"Well, I've got all day, and don't you dare tell me you loved her. It was everything but love," I replied quickly.

He took another deep breath as if it were his last inhalation on earth. "I tried my best. . . ." he said. His face began to change as if he were holding something within, something big, like a whole new galaxy waiting to be explored, or maybe it was something a lot worse. Who knew? All I knew was that there was something mysterious in his eyes, something dangerous. He was like a man with everything to gain and nothing to lose. A man with lost dreams, lost love, and lost hope, a man with nothing to live for.

"You tried your best?" I asked, using an amused tone of voice as if I were surprised. I couldn't believe what I was hearing. I know it was a bit harsh and sarcastic of me, but like I mentioned before, perhaps he didn't deserve my sympathy, at least not yet.

"I tried, I really did. I tried to be there for her, but I couldn't." His words stumbled as he tried to catch them.

"You couldn't? How? I just don't understand." It was indeed a little too hard to believe. I mean, how could you possibly try? Perhaps he hadn't tried hard enough. You couldn't possibly try to do anything without a little effort. It didn't connect for me, and by that I meant that if he had really wanted to be there, he would have been there, because in the end, what on earth can possibly stop anyone from doing what they want to do in the first place? I didn't see eye to eye with what he had just said. It didn't make any sense.

"I'm sorry; I just find it hard to believe," I repeated steadily as I shook my head. By now the waitress had returned with our beverages.

"Thank you, dear," he said to the waitress as she filled his cup with coffee. He sighed. He picked up his coffee and began to stir it using the silver spoon next to him.

"Are you two ready to order?" she asked.

"Give us a minute, dear," he said, and she nodded and took a few steps back, disappearing into the background.

"I know you're angry and I know Harper meant a lot to you. She meant a lot to me, too." He lifted his left hand and slowly blew onto his cup of coffee. He was right about one thing: Harper did mean the world to me. She was my best friend and I would have given my very own life to have one more night with her. I was defensive. I felt as if I still had to protect her from people, even those she loved.

"I don't know how to start this, so I'm just going to tell it how it is." I didn't say a word. My eyes were open, and my ears and hands were loose as if I was preparing myself for the worst. Again, I didn't know what to expect. I mean, this man could tell me anything and it was up to me to believe it or not.

"There were many times where I tried to see Harper, many times, and every time I went to see her, her mother would cover it all up with lies. She would say that Harper didn't want to see me and vice versa. She made me seem like the bad guy when in truth, it was her. Everything was because of her mother, and every reason why I suddenly disappeared was that she manipulated it." His hands began to shake gently. He frowned and his eyes fell as if they were far too heavy to hold up. He was shaken up a bit, and the way his voice trembled made it sound distorted by what he had said.

I was curious now. Real or not, I needed to know exactly what had happened between the two of them. Although I knew it wasn't my business, I still felt as if it was something I needed to know. I began to calm myself. I began to take breaths and focus.

"What did she do?" I asked as he paused for a few seconds. I guess he was trying to collect himself, trying to remember the past.

"She did everything in her power to cover up the truth. I guess in her mind, she didn't want Harper growing up hating her, so she influenced Harper to hate me instead—"

"She didn't hate you. It was everything but hate, believe me," I said before he could even finish his sentence. "She loved you, she really loved you, and you abandoned her. You know, I rehearsed this moment many times in my head," I said. "And every time I thought about seeing you in person, if ever, I would play it all out using my imagination. I wanted to tell you how much you really damaged her and how much I hated you for that, and now, sitting here next to you, I just can't seem to do that. I don't know if I hate you or feel sorry for you. I don't know if I feel sorry for you because you never had the chance to know Harper as I did."

For years I had stayed up late with Harper, for years I had seen her sob over guys, and for years none of her worries ever compared with the pain her father had left her with, the pain she held and lived with every day. My pain couldn't compare with the kind of hurting Harper had gone through. This of course was something I thought about over and over. I was a broken record of things, of moments, thoughts, and feelings. And by all means, Harper's pain and the significant vanishing of her father was something I thought about even more after her death. It was just one of those things.

"You must hate me," he said.

"No, I thought I did, but I don't hate you. Harper didn't, so I don't either. I just wish things weren't as they were. So, what else happened? Tell me the truth; it's all we have, you know?" I took a slurp off my Dr Pepper.

"The truth is, in short"—he took a deep breath and continued—"Harper's mother cheated on me when Harper was a little girl. I forgave her, and then she did it again and I forgave her a second time. She was afraid I'd legally take Harper away from her," he said calmly.

There was literally nothing I could have said after that. After all, Harper's mother was somewhat mysterious too. She had barely been around, and sometimes she had been so secretive that Harper herself would question her activities. I remembered this because every other weekend she, too, would disappear, but unlike her father, she did return home.

"She kept cheating on me and eventually, I got tired of it. I was going to take her to court for full custody of Harper. She was unfit to be a mother. She had a lot of issues, especially with alcohol. The day I talked to her about it, she and I got in a really bad argument and she called the cops on me. She lied to them and said I was abusive, and because of that, I had to move out. She even hurt herself and said it was me, and because of it, soon after, she placed a restraining order on me. Go figure. She said I was violent and that I was unfit to be a father and how unhealthy I was for Harper's development. We took it all to court, and of course they gave her full custody of Harper. Soon after, something ticked inside of me. I made uncountable attempts to see her, and every time I did, I went to jail. That lasted a few years. To this day I don't understand how Harper never noticed my several arrests in front of where she lived." He said it with a faraway stare as if he were watching a film behind me about his past.

"It's funny, you know?" he said.

"Yeah," I replied.

"Her mother was this monster and she took all her faults and threw them toward me. She turned me into a monster, and all I wanted was to see my little girl. I tried so hard to be there for her, but I couldn't. It was a nightmare for me. Eventually, I moved back to San Francisco, and every so often I would visit, but I wouldn't knock on the door, I wouldn't demand to see her as I had done before. All I would do was wait to see if I could catch Harper outside. That's all I wanted. I just wanted to see her, to tell her I was still here, that I still loved her no matter what." A tear fell from his eye, but he quickly wiped it with the napkin that was unfolded on his lap. He didn't sob. He held it in, but you could see from the corner of his eye that everything that had ever hurt him was still there, waiting to surface like a balloon trapped beneath the ocean.

He continued and I kept on listening. It was the only thing I could do. "After that, I wrote her a letter every day, all the way till her death. And as I wrote them, I kept getting them back in the mail. Harper's mother would send them back as refused."

As he spoke, I began to think, *Every time I was here, her grave site was covered with envelopes, and they were always scattered in every direction. It was the same type of envelope he placed over her tombstone just moments ago.* It was beginning to make sense.

"All of those have been yours right? I've seen them lying around."

"Yes, I place one every day. I have thousands."

"So every day you leave a letter you wrote for her from before on her grave? The same letters you had been writing for over a decade?"

"Yes."

"So what will you do when you run out of letters?" I know it was insensitive of me and unsympathetic to ask, but I did it anyway. Something inside of me felt sad. I wanted to cry, but the tears didn't find their way out. I felt so bad inside. I felt terrible being here in front of her father, knowing that all he'd wanted the entire time was the same thing I wanted for Harper: to make sure she was okay, to make sure she was loved, and most of all, to make sure she was happy.

"I'll continue to write her letters every day for the rest of my life." When he said that, it struck me.

Here he was, a broken man, perhaps even more broken than I was, leaving the past on Harper's resting site. What hurt me even more was that the entire time Harper believed he'd forgotten her, that he probably had more children of his own and that he probably loved them more than he did her. But that wasn't the case. He was a man, one filled with love, and all he had wanted was to catch his little girl out in the wild, laughing and smiling with her friends. You had to be a real monster to prevent that from happening. I couldn't believe it, but it was probably true. Something in my gut was telling me it was.

"All I think about was how alone she must have felt after she discovered her disease," he added as another tear slipped from his eye. "She must have been calling out for me, you know. It's entirely my fault."

Ironically, that was the same exact way I felt. I felt as if I had let her down, as if I had let her die. It was all my fault. *I could have done more; I know I could have saved her,* I thought as I put myself back together. And then something he had just said struck me. She had a disease? Had I heard that correctly or was my mind playing tricks on me?

"Excuse me, but you just said—"

"She was sick about three years or so before her death. She discovered she was sick."

"What do you mean she was sick?" I hesitated to ask, but it was unbelievable. I mean, I was her best friend. If she'd been sick, I would have known. She wouldn't have kept something like that away from me, something that serious. What the hell was going on?

"What do you mean she was sick?" I was in denial. My voice got high-pitched and my blood was beginning to boil. I wasn't exactly sure what was happening here. I mean, she was sick? No, no, she wasn't. She was fine; she was just hormonal, or going through some sort of strange phase. I mean, anything but sick. She wasn't sick! As I thought, my heart began to pound. How could someone say she was sick?

"Oh, Wes," he said sincerely as he frowned. "Harper had Lou Gehrig's disease. It was very aggressive that year of her death."

My thoughts began to stutter. I couldn't believe it. No, I couldn't allow it. I cleared my throat as I tried to put two and two together. I shook my head, and then my eyes widened as if I were trying to see a picture in a dark room. "No, no, that can't be true. That can't be right. I would have known. No, none of this is making any sense right now. No, I'm sorry, I don't believe you. No."

"It's the truth, dear. She was very ill."

"No, I can't allow that. I'm sorry."

"It was a surprise for me, too," he said. "I found out only after her death. Her mother showed me all the medical exams and papers to prove it."

I didn't want to believe it. There was no way she would have kept that from me, from us. Suddenly, I was beginning to feel dizzy, as if I had to throw up. I was light-headed. I wanted to faint— to wake up from this nightmare. My hands were shaking, and I was beginning to have random muscle spasms. My chest felt heavy, and I was having difficulty breathing.

"Excuse me, but I need to get up. I need some—" I couldn't compile my thoughts correctly; it was as if everything I'd ever known was a lie. Imagine that, discovering everything for the first time and all at once. It was a little too much to bear.

"Wes, wait—" he said as I suddenly lifted myself from the chair and quickly paced outside.

I needed a moment. I needed some fresh air. I needed someone, anyone, to tell me it was going to be okay. It was a lot to take in at once; it was too much to handle, too much for me to keep my composure. I almost fell walking out. I tripped over my own shoe. I was that delusional, out of my element. I wanted to break into a million pieces. I wanted to disappear while I was standing in front of the water. I wanted to dissolve into the air and travel toward some place where I didn't know a thing.

I stood outside by the railings alone, scared and confused. I felt betrayed. I felt angry, even more so than before, but not with Harper. I was angry with myself. I was angry for not realizing anything, and for the first time in a long time, I felt as if I needed Owen, the only person who would understand what I was going through. I began to sob. I was sitting on the ground with both my hands over my face. The tears pierced through my hands and landed on the ground. One followed the other, and before I knew it, I was sobbing quietly by myself without care.

I couldn't stop. It was as if I had a chain of sadness and the outcome was an undefined amount of pain. But it wasn't just any kind of pain, it was real pain, and not the kind of pain you feel when you lose someone. No, it was the kind of pain you feel when you lose yourself and watch yourself from below as who you once were passes by.

I continued to sob, and I wasn't sure if I was going to stop. I mean, it hurt. It hurt more than before. It hurt worse than when she died or when I left him behind. All of it. All of it hurt the way it should have. It hurt the way all things hurt when you believe they're yours. It all came down again and I was buried beneath it. Why did this happen? Why did she have to die? Why did I abandon the man I love?

Today had been such an emotional day. I couldn't take any more. I just couldn't. I must have stayed there for over an hour. I never saw Harper's father after that. I never went back looking for him, and I never saw him walk out, either. I just stayed there, lifeless, as if I were waiting for someone to come pick me up and put me back together again.

14

The next day I woke up later than usual. The clock on the nightstand said it was 9:58 in the morning. Most of the time while here, I would wake up bright and early to prepare myself for my flight back home. Sometimes, although it was rare, I would decide at the last minute to stay an extra day or two, but like I said, it wasn't too often. This time, I just wanted to go home. I wanted to take a time-out from everything and everyone, maybe even a long vacation from myself.

I had had a hard time sleeping the night before, and because of that, I'd had to take 20 milligrams of melatonin. At times, I took some pills to help ease me down, to help me fall asleep when I needed to. I must have slept over ten hours. I was still a tad drowsy.

I stayed at the Westin. It was near the financial district by Union Square. I didn't want anyone to bother me, so I had turned my phone off. It felt good being in complete solitude, at least for the time being. It felt refreshing and reminded me of easier times. Maybe I needed that. Maybe I just needed some sleep. Sometimes a good night's rest is enough to reset your entire mind frame, your entire way of thinking.

All it takes is one night; one night is enough to change the wiring in your brain. One night is enough to reprogram everything, feelings and all. But obviously, for me, it was easier said than done.

Today, I woke up sad, gloomy, and somewhat disturbed. I woke up stiff and lazy. I woke up wanting to float away, wanting to get swallowed alive by the future I didn't know I had.

I got up to wash my face. The hotel's floor was cold, and the room was even colder. I tiptoed to the restroom with a chill. It ran down my spine while both of my arms shivered violently. I turned on the lights; they were really bright. I squinted until my eyes focused. I couldn't keep them open as I walked. It was quiet; all you heard was the loud rumble coming from the air conditioner. It sounded like a semi-truck passing through the street.

I stood there. I stood there in front of the sink, watching my reflection from the mirror before me. I didn't move. I didn't blink. I didn't yawn. I didn't stretch any of my limbs. My teeth were clattering, and every ten seconds or so I shivered. All I had on were my undergarments. My hair was a mess, my head was still pounding, and my face was swollen to the point where I barely recognized myself.

I stood there, lifeless, as I opened my eyes to see if they had cleared up from the vast amount of sobbing I had done the night before. I didn't want to jump on board a plane and have every passenger stare at me. I hated that kind of attention. I didn't deserve it, nor did I want it.

My eyes were sore, too sore; it was as if each retinal vein had exploded within the white space of my eyes. I felt like shit. I felt as if I had gone drinking the night before and had had more than I could handle. Maybe I should have had some drinks; at least it would have explained why I had been sobbing all night. I mean, this had been a hell of a week for me. It's not like I didn't expect it, because yes, every time I came to visit Harper's grave, I was a bit more emotional and anxious than usual that week, but could you blame me? I was going to see my best friend, one who no longer inhabited the earth, one I missed beyond control. Because of it, I think I was allowed to be a little emotional. I think I was allowed to feel like shit more than on any other day of the year, and I also think it was okay for me to shed tears throughout the night. It was only fair.

I thought about what Harper's father had said. It played over and over throughout the night. The thing was, I wasn't sure if I even wanted to know about Harper's illness. I wasn't sure if that was how I wanted to leave San Francisco, with another chapter to add to her story, and I wasn't sure I wanted to believe it. I mean, would I have been better off not knowing? After all, ignorance is bliss, isn't it? Did I have to know? What difference would it have made? Perhaps none, absolutely nothing, because in the end, she still wasn't here and nothing was ever going to bring her back.

But apart from that, it all made a little sense now. That was another thing that struck me: how sometimes I had felt while she was alive that she was hiding something but I wasn't brave enough to ask her. I guess in a lot of ways, I was a bad friend—a terrible one to be exact. I hadn't even seen it coming. At the moment, all I had seen was Harper's behavior shifting and I had done nothing to help her in her demise.

Nonetheless, as soon as I arrived home, I had some researching to do, I thought. I mean, someone back home must have known something. Someone back home must have somewhat of an explanation or recognition or a clue, anything, to at least confirm what Harper's father had told me the day before. It was hard enough to believe, but at this point anything was possible and I could have believed anyone, anything, really. I mean, I needed answers, and it didn't matter where they came from as long as they arrived in such a way that eased the pain. That's all.

I slowly walked back toward the bed. I covered myself with the blanket I'd been using and sank my head between the two large pillows in the middle of the bed. I was comfortable—zoned out but ultimately comfortable. I was contemplating what to do. I had some time to kill. I was thinking of maybe visiting Harper's grave one last time before I left. I felt as if I hadn't really spent enough time with her because of the encounter I had had with her father. I had about five hours or so until I jumped back on a plane. I wasn't looking forward to it, but with everything that was going through my mind, the flight seemed microscopic, as if it didn't matter. That was the least of my concerns.

I kept thinking about Harper and Owen. I thought about my life and how it had turned out. I thought about the decisions I had made and whether they were the right ones. I thought about my mother and my father and why they were divorced to begin with. I thought about home. I thought about whether home was really my home and if home was a place or a person. I thought about everything, from as far as I could remember to what had happened yesterday with Harper's father. Was it rude of me to do such a thing to him, leave without even saying good-bye? The same way Harper left me behind without a single word to hang on to or the same way I left Owen without a proper explanation?

I thought about life, and how life was a series of events, both arriving and leaving, saying both good-bye and hello. And how maybe everyone I had ever loved wasn't meant to stay with me forever. How maybe everyone I had ever loved was temporarily with me for a reason, one I probably would never have the blessing to know. Or maybe I was just naïve enough to believe that.

Maybe I still had a lot to learn and a lot of growing up to do. I mean, I was broken, and at times, thinking was all I did. Maybe it was moments like these when I needed them the most— when I needed my best friends to tell me everything was going to be okay. I hated these moments. I hated feeling alone. I hated that my best friend was buried in the ground and the love of my life was nowhere to be found.

I was on the mattress for an extra thirty minutes before I had the energy to get back up. I slid out of the bed as if my body were made of sand. I couldn't remember what I had been doing before those thoughts. I must have fallen asleep. I yawned and stretched my limbs as far as I could. The room was still cold. I turned over and grabbed my phone and turned it on. There were no text messages, no missed calls; there was nothing from anyone I knew. I could have died and no one would have noticed. I didn't think anything of it, although it was a little unusual that neither my mother nor my father had called me since last night, considering they were both about three thousand miles from where I currently was.

I walked into the bathroom and began to change. It was now almost 11:00 a.m. My flight was at 4:00 p.m., meaning I had to arrive at the airport by 3:00 at the latest. I quickly got dressed. I was wearing my dark blue jeans and a black tank, accompanied by aviator sunglasses to cover my worn eyes. I grabbed my belongings and checked out at the lobby. I was preparing myself again because I was going to visit Harper one last time before I headed back home.

I was looking forward to it as always. At times, I felt as if I could be by her side for a lifetime, lying there next to her tombstone, watching my life pass me by. Other times I wanted to get as far away as possible. I guess it was all based on my mood, and right now I just needed her, I just needed Harper to be there, alive or not.

I was walking out of Starbucks. I can't stress enough how much I needed coffee. It was around the corner from the hotel. I walked toward the edge of the street for a cab. It was cloudy and cool outside. This San Francisco weather was something to die for. Every time I was here, it was perfect, from the weather to the food. It all made me feel at ease. Sometimes I thought about moving here. I mean, apart from Harper being here, there was something welcoming and inspiring about San Francisco. Everything felt real, alive, and full of color. I really don't know what it was, to be honest, but it felt good, and the more I came, the more I wanted to stay. In a lot of ways, yes, every time I came here it was sad, but it was also a beautiful experience, a very satisfying one, as if I had been starved for something I needed but had no clue what it was and living here would fill my soul.

I also got to learn a little more about myself each time. I got to understand my nightmares, my fears, and anything else that placed a weight on my life, but when I left, of course, as I mentioned before, everything would eventually go back to what it was. With time, everything would ultimately reveal itself again, and too often I would find myself back in the gloom of things.

I paid the cabdriver the last few dollars I had. The ride hadn't been too bad. The cabdriver kept telling me I looked beautiful, and he kept telling these ridiculous old jokes that weren't funny at all. I guess he was trying to make me laugh—that, or trying to get a bigger tip. He kept asking me why I was so quiet after his awful jokes. Most of the drive he tried to make small talk. I barely spoke. I wasn't in the mood to talk or be friendly.

I was a bit tired and I was only thinking of the flight back home, the long, treacherous flight back home. Apart from the jokes and small talk I did appreciate the last thing the cabdriver told me before I got out. I think he said this because I was being dropped off in a cemetery. In his foreign accent he said something that stuck to me as if it were something I was meant to hear.

Maybe it was even a sign. The way he said it was even more haunting because he looked back and his dark brown eyes pierced through my sunglasses. It was as if he was looking directly into my soul, talking to my heart and giving me the strength I needed to do what I had come to do.

He said with a slow, gentle intensity,

"Before you go, I want to tell you something. You can take this however you want." The cab came to a complete stop in front of Woodlawn Memorial Park. "I want to tell you that everyone has this force, this gravity, this pull, this attraction. And this force becomes stronger between people who are separated by distance or even death. Some may say it's the emotional connection, that feeling of missing someone, but I don't think it's that. I think people are meant to meet. I think the people who are in our lives are because of this force, the one we all obtain as we gravitate toward each other. And this force or whatever it is gets stronger as time goes on. What I'm trying to say is, whoever you're missing will find you again. Maybe not in this lifetime, but in the next. Whoever it is, you will be reunited once again."

I almost began to cry as he shared this with me. It was the sharpest thing anyone had said to me in a very long time. It was comforting but it also hurt. It was sensitive, and yet it was harsh enough to break you into a million pieces. The reality of losing the beloved was perhaps the hardest thing in the world to go through. I couldn't find a proper response to what the cabdriver said. All I said in response was thank you. It was the only thing that came to my mind.

As I entered the park, I noticed from afar that someone was standing by Harper's grave. I instantly thought it was her father, someone I didn't want to run into again. Because of that, I entered the gift shop to kill some time. I paced around for several minutes, contemplating and waiting till the man left. I peeked out several times, but he was still there, motionless, like a frozen statue above her grave. He was wearing a black trench coat and a black hat to go with it. He was smoking a cigarette, and he kept moving his left hand in and out of his pocket. I was waiting so long that I even bought Harper some flowers to make up for having arrived empty-handed yesterday. I bought her some pink daisies. They were her favorite, growing up, and I knew she would appreciate them from the other side.

I kept waiting. The man didn't budge. It didn't seem like he was going anywhere anytime soon. I was getting anxious. I continued to pace around the gift shop. Time was ticking, a vital part of my trip. Eventually I had to go, although something inside of me was telling me to stay for a few more days. This time, I couldn't. I mean, Thanksgiving was two days from now, and I had agreed to spend it in New York City with my father.

I kept peeking through the edge of the gift shop window. The employees in the shop must have thought I was insane. I grunted and stomped my feet. "Shit," I whispered to myself. I really didn't want to run into her father again. "Shit," I whispered again. I had nothing to say to that man. I looked at my watch. An entire twenty-five minutes had passed. Now I was in for it. I had to do it. I had to make a decision. I had to go and talk to him. *"Shit,"* I said out loud. I had to go, and it wasn't for myself but for Harper. I had to do it for her. I mean, if I didn't, then I wouldn't be able to live with myself. I knew if I didn't go then, that would be another stress, and I already had a handful of them to deal with on my own.

I grabbed her flowers and exited the gift shop. I beamed out of there and headed straight toward Harper's resting place. I gave in. I had no other option. I took my time getting there, though, one step after the other in a single line until I reached her—him. I took one breath after the other until I came to a complete stop. I didn't make a sound. I was standing right behind him. He wasn't startled. He slowly turned around, and in that moment my heart flew out of my chest like a wild bird flying through the rain.

"Wes, is that you?" he said in a deep, rough voice as he faced me. It was him. It was the other one. The one I ran away from. The one I loved but didn't know how to love. It was the man my heart belonged to, the man who claimed all of my skies and silenced all of my demons.

He was here, standing before me, after all those years, after all those long, sad, terrible years. We stood five feet from one another. And I wasn't sure if I wanted to collapse into his arms or have him suddenly fall into mine. I could tell he was taken aback by the way he stood. He was shaken, and perhaps, like me, he was wondering if I was really there, if this was all a mirage and he had made me up in his head.

"Owen," I said as every letter of his name pierced through my skin, through my soul. *Am I dreaming?* I thought as I closed my eyes, hoping that in some way, somehow, time would retaliate and stand still. "Are you really here?" I whispered to myself. Sadly, I couldn't trust my eyes, let alone my heart.

15

In the midst of it all, I was right in front of someone I once knew. He existed somewhere in the world, but I had long forgotten what it felt like to see his face. It had been that long. He was unrecognizable, but I knew it was him. He looked different, but he had the same unforgettable sunken eyes, the ones I fell into when I was nothing more than a young girl. He smelled the same too. There was only one person on this earth that smelled like him, like all the summers we shared together and all the rainy days we spent running in circles chasing our dreams.

You know, life is strange, because I had always envisioned this very moment. I had always wondered what I would say or how I would act if I ever ran into him. A lot of times, I knew exactly what I was going to say and do, but now, seeing him in front of me in the flesh made my mind go blank.

I just never, for the life of me, had expected this to happen, especially here. I mean, I wanted it to happen but not like this. Not here, not in front of Harper's grave. I wasn't ready to see him, but then again, who's ever ready for this kind of encounter? No matter when this very moment happened—now or ten years from now—I probably would never have been ready for it.

His face was furrowed by age but still sculpted. His skin was weather beaten but still young and alive. It was surreal, seeing him in front of me. It was unimaginable, and everything around me was moving in slow motion. I had almost forgotten what he looked like, but it all came back to me suddenly. He was tall and athletic, and beneath his black coat he wore a dark green button-down with a black tie. He looked good—older, mature, and with a single glance I was his once again.

He stood firmly before me. He softly smiled and had this distinct look in his eyes, as if the entire world had gone silent. For a brief moment we didn't spill any words. We just looked at one another, smiling as if we held a secret from our surroundings. I smiled back and I did it with ease. It came off naturally, without thinking about what I was going to do or think next.

"It's been a long time, Wes," he said as he embraced me with another warm smile. It gave me goose bumps. It made me feel as if I was the only person in the world, and for a moment, I felt sad. I felt sympathetic and I felt alone. I also felt bad, really bad, because in that very moment, I also remembered the last time I had seen him and how harsh I had been to him. All those feelings came to me suddenly and our last memory tickled the back of my neck as if it had happened just yesterday. I remembered his face, that last look he gave me, a hopeless, exhausted look. That alone made it unbearable for me to look him in the eyes.

I was almost embarrassed about all the pain I might have caused him. With every breath, I wanted to hide. I was that ashamed. I also felt sorry for him and for myself because of all the unfortunate surprises life had thrown at us without properly preparing us for their outcome. Ironically enough, he was here in the last place I would ever have expected to bump into him. But of course, that's how life was; at least that's how it was for me. In fact, I wasn't sure why by now; I still didn't expect the unexpected. I mean, for me, so many things happen at random that this should have been clearly foreseeable. This should have been in the cards.

"Yes, yes, it has been," I said, and looked toward the ground as if I were looking for a place to hide. I suddenly brushed my left hand against my hair as every atom in my body screamed. I was hurt that I hadn't spoken to or seen him in years and I wasn't sure what I wanted or what to feel. I mean, one second I wanted to tell him how much I missed him, how much I still loved him, and how much I had thought about him every day since the last time we had spoken.

I wanted to tell him I was sorry, that I was sorry for everything, including Harper's death. I had so much to say, and I didn't have the time to say it. In another second I just wanted to run away, not say a single thing, and disappear again.

"You look different," I said to him. It was the only thing that came to my mind apart from the chaos within.

"Yeah, you do too, but in a good way," he said.

I smiled gently as I took off my sunglasses. "So here we are," I said, extending both of my arms as if I were confused.

"Yeah . . ." He looked down at Harper's grave, and then he turned back toward me.

"Some life, right?" I added as he looked down toward the ground and placed his right hand behind his neck. He chuckled slightly as he did so.

"Yeah, some life."

"So, you come here too?" I knew it was ridiculous to even ask, because of course I knew he would visit her from time to time. That was obvious. I mean, he loved her just as much as I did. She was like a sister to him, to us; not coming here wouldn't have made much sense considering how much we all meant to one another.

"Of course, every year since."

"Yeah . . . me too." There was a sudden pause as the Pacific wind blew across our faces.

"You know, I think about her every night," he admitted, as if he wasn't sure if I was going to be there the next minute. He just went for it, and it was obvious we were going to have this conversation as soon as we bumped heads. I'm sure, like me, he had been expecting it to happen one day.

"So do I."

"I also think about you," he said as if he were confessing to me. There was so much of him in the air.

I inhaled him in and confessed a little as well. "So do I," I replied, and then he began to talk. Slowly he began to open up and tell me almost everything I needed to hear. The only issue was that I wasn't sure if he was too late or I was. I wasn't sure if now was the right moment, but then again, there was never a right moment, not for matters of the heart. It was now or never, at least that's how it felt. Maybe he was being too intrusive and straightforward, but I guess we both had this understanding that maybe we would never see each other again, and because of that, then perhaps we wanted to get as much as we could out of the short amount of time we both probably already knew we didn't have.

"I think about everything, from our childhood to the last night I saw you, Wes. Not a night goes by when I don't think of you," he said calmly. I'd thought I was the only one. Clearly I wasn't, and hearing him say so made me feel a lot less like a wreck and a little more normal, a little more vulnerable, and a little more human.

"So do I." My voice trembled. Patiently enough, I knew where this conversation was headed, and like I mentioned, we were long overdue for this.

"You know, I know maybe this isn't the right time, but I almost lost my mind when you left. I thought I was going to die. I thought I was going to end up in a mental institution. I just felt lost without you, Wes." He chuckled again as if it were all just one giant misunderstanding, as if he knew it was meant to happen and he was okay with it.

Maybe to him, it was all too funny or all too sad, sad enough to laugh about it. I smirked slightly as if I, too, felt the same way about the situation, about everything, because I, too, had felt as if I were going mad, as if I was never meant to recover from the entire thing he and Harper gave me, as if all the love, all the laughter, and all the memories were agents of death sent to kill me.

"It's funny, you know," he said.

"Yeah, it is."

"Like when we were kids, I never intended for anything like this to happen, and when it did, I was a different person overnight. I didn't even know who I was, and I spent a countless amount of time trying to figure it out, trying to see how to win you back, but then, I couldn't even figure that out either."

I stood there motionless. I felt the same way, because when Harper died, I thought I no longer knew who I was or who I wanted to be. I no longer knew anything. It was as if my entire life had no connection with my present life. My life was a rolling movie projector without film in the cartridge. Like an empty narrative filled with meaningless words and stanzas with no particular definition or reason at all. And when I left Owen, it became worse—I became worse. My life and everything I thought defined me became this blank canvas, this floating seed with nowhere to go.

"I guess what I'm trying to say is, I miss you, Wes. I really do, and I don't know who I am without you."

As he spoke I began to feel something stirring within me. I began to feel nauseated. I felt as if I was experiencing a terrible headache, but I wasn't. I tilted my head and opened my eyes, frowned, and then shook my head. I remembered, and I wanted to know if he knew anything about it.

"Did you know about Harper?" I suddenly asked. The question came out of me like a cannonball piercing a brick wall. I knew maybe that wasn't the right thing to ask, at least not right now, but it was the only thing I thought of. Not that I didn't want to continue the dialogue—I mean, I missed him too, tremendously—it was just that I needed to know if he had heard anything. And if he had, then I wanted to know what he knew.

"What do you mean?" Obviously he'd been caught off guard. I guess he wasn't expecting me to cut him off like that, let alone ask such a question.

"I ran into her father here yesterday."

"What! You did? How?"

"Yeah, I was here, and then he showed up, we talked for a while, and then we had lunch, and then he said something that kind of made me fall flat on my face."

"And what was that? What did he say to you?"

"He said"—I fumbled a little—"he said she was sick, that she had been sick a few years before she died, and that the year she died she became *really* sick, and then I kind of overreacted and left, because I couldn't believe it. I mean, how could I have not known? I was her best friend. More than anyone, I would have known. I don't know, but nothing is making any sense right now." I was a bit confused and slightly shaken up.

"Oh . . ." He paused and placed one of his hands over his head. His hand twitched back and forth as if he were scratching his hair. He then sighed as if he were the bearer of bad news, as if he had known all this time.

"She was sick, Wes. She was very ill," he said carefully.

"So you knew?"

"Yes—well, no, not exactly. I found out not too long ago, from a friend of her family. Maybe six or seven months ago."

I suddenly dropped the bouquet of flowers I held in my hands out of shock. For a moment, I felt betrayed again, or maybe it was disappointment. At the moment, I couldn't differentiate between the two. One thing was certain, though: I felt isolated, as if I had been left on an island to die. I couldn't believe it, I just couldn't. If I hadn't arrived here at the right time, at the right moment, I wouldn't have run into Harper's father, and I wouldn't have known she was sick. I'd been hoping all last night that it was some kind of misunderstanding. I mean, after all, her father hadn't been around, so how would he have *really* known, despite what he'd said about reconnecting with Harper's mother?

Of course, I tried to make sense of it. That was all I knew to do. If something didn't make any sense to me, I would find something to clarify it, even if it wasn't true. I guess I was undeniably selfish, in doubt of everything. I didn't want to accept the truth. The truth was always hard to forget and hard to tell. The truth, at times, hurt no matter what, and the more I thought about it, the more the world faded into the nothingness of it all, and I felt even more alone than before.

I took a deep breath as I picked up Harper's flowers.

"I'm sorry you had to find out this way," Owen said. "I really don't know anything about it. No one really knew, I think. It's one of those things, you know?"

I found the courage within me to relax a little. And yes, it was one of those things, the kind of thing that I knew I would take with me to my very own grave, the kind of thing that would probably keep me up at night for the next few months or so. And last but not least, it was the kind of thing I didn't want to remember about her but knew I couldn't forget.

"Yeah, you're right. Whether it was a lie or the truth, nothing is going to bring her back," I said as I stood back up and wiped the dirt off the flowers with my hand. As I stood, I almost lost control, but again, I held it in. My heart was racing and my mind had become a playground for all the demons that reminded me of our past. It had been such an emotional week for me, and I was still exhausted, too exhausted, and by now all I really wanted to do was lie in my bed back home.

"I, I have to go," I said as I turned around, taking a few steps back. That was it; I'd had enough. I had finally reached my breaking point. After feeling too much, thinking too much, and being reminded of all the things that hurt, all I wanted was to be left alone. I was done talking, worrying, stressing, and crying. At this point, all I wanted was to wait in the airport terminal till I boarded my flight back home.

"Wes, c'mon, I just saw you. Please don't go."

I halted. I stood there facing the exit, facing away from the people I still loved, then looked down. "Will this ever stop? Will this ever end? Will I eventually become who I was?" I whispered to myself, but it was loud enough for Owen to hear me.

"I don't know. . . ." he said. I heard him sigh. I guess in that moment he finally realized that what we'd once had no longer existed. He knew he had no influence on me. If I wanted to go, I would, and there was nothing he could say or do to stop me. But of course, I stayed. I didn't move. I guess a small part of me still belonged to him, and it was a part of me neither one of us knew how to grasp.

"I know what you're going through, Wes, believe me, I really do, but running away every time you're confronted with something that puts you in a difficult position isn't going to help you. You know that." He took a step closer to me.

He was right. He was always right at some point, and I hated that. I knew that if I left now, I would probably regret it forever.

"Yes, I know, you're right."

"Wes?"

I couldn't hold it anymore. I began sobbing, but it was a different kind of sobbing. It was as if everyone I knew had suddenly vanished and I was locked in an empty room, in an empty world. Every fiber of my being began to ache. Every muscle, every tissue, and every organ somewhat felt my hurting. Even my bones were in pain, and the pain radiated from the middle of the marrow.

It was as if my skeleton had fallen in hot magma. I was on fire. I felt this terrible burning, beginning from the core of my body and exiting right through my hair follicles. I had never felt such an intense feeling. I turned around to face Owen and began to shatter and shatter and shatter. I shattered a thousand times, over and over. The sky had fallen, the moon, the stars, and the clouds.

"You think this is easy for me?" I said. "Do you even know what it's like? I don't know anything. I don't know who I am, and I'm not running. I never was. Not from you or Harper's death or anything. I'm trying to live. I'm trying to be happy again, but I can't. Don't you see? I can't be happy when everyone I once loved can't be allowed into my heart anymore. And it's like I'm locked out but also locked in. I'm trapped between two worlds. I want to keep you and I want to let go, and I love you and I don't at the very same time."

I was filled with tears. It was obvious that the light within my soul had gone dim, that the candle in my heart had been incinerated into ash. If there was any kind of revelation for me, now would be the perfect time for it to reveal itself. I was desperate. I needed it. I needed something to give me back my confidence, my will, and my desire to live a normal life. I needed some kind of aid to help me reevaluate myself and make sense of all these choices that had led me to this uncontrolled sadness.

Owen came closer. He stopped right in front of me and sighed. He placed both of his warm hands on my arms. "Wes . . ." He said my name as if I was his savior, and I looked into his eyes as if he were mine. "You know, since I've known you, I've never had the right words for you. And to be honest, I probably never will, but something brought us here together. Maybe it's something none of us can see, at least not now. And I know you're upset and I know you probably don't want to see me."

He was wrong. I did want to see him, I did want to sit down and talk, but not here, not like this. It wasn't the right time, and my mind was too distorted to reason with anything.

"I'm sorry," Owen said. "I'm sorry for all the harm that has passed your way. I'm sorry for all those nights you had to go through this alone. I'm sorry for the way you feel empty, for the way you feel lost and hopeless. I'm sorry for not being there for you. I wish I could take the suffering away, I really do, Wes." He sounded sincere, and his tone inspired more tears to fall out of my eyes.

I felt broken, perhaps even more than I had the night before. And then, it came out—the only question I had for him. It was, in a lot of ways, the root of all my questions, and it wasn't about Harper. No, it didn't even involve her, for my question was more about us than anything. I looked deep into his eyes as if I was looking through a glass door, and as I did, he glued his eyes back to mine as if there wasn't another moment to spare.

"Why didn't you come looking for me?" I said as my eyes swung toward the ground. That was it. That was everything. Why hadn't he come to find me? Why hadn't he cared enough to see how I was doing? To see if I was okay?

"Why didn't you come find me?" I persisted. It was not that I was demanding an answer. It was more that I wanted to understand why, even if the truth hurt. I mean, if I was the love of his life, why had he let me go so easily? Why hadn't he fought for me, for us, in my time of need? From my understanding, love made people move mountains, drain oceans, clear deserts if they were the obstacles to true love.

"Just tell me why," I repeated. Maybe I was demanding something, some kind of explanation.

He took two steps away from me, paced around, and then came back toward me like the ocean sliding across the shore. "I don't know. . . ." he said as he put one of his hands in his pocket.

"You don't know?" It took him several moments to respond. Of course, he was probably gathering his feelings together. After all, it had been two long years, and he probably didn't know, or at least, he didn't know how to express it. Suddenly, he stood and blurted half a word, but it didn't come out fully. It was as if he was holding something within, something that was too hard to say. I stood in front of him, zoning in and out of his eyes, zoning in and out of Harper's grave, out of the sky and the tree behind Owen.

"Because," he muttered quietly.

"Because what, Owen?"

"Because it was the right thing to do," he said.

"How could you possibly think that way?" My words came out rapidly. "Because it was the right thing to do? I needed you. I needed you to come save me, to come look for me, to fight for me, to come show me that maybe someone still cared. I just needed you, Owen. I needed you and now, now it's too late."

My heart began to break in pieces before him. It was true; I hadn't wanted to deal with it alone. Although it was my decision to leave, I still needed him to stop me. I needed him to tell me how wrong I was. I needed him to grab me by the hand and tell me I wasn't alone. How he would be there for me, grieving the loss of my best friend. But no, that's not how it went down. I left, and left for my very own reasons, and still, all Owen did was watch me go. He did nothing. He didn't do enough, at least enough for me to stay.

"Wes, I'm not here to argue. I let you go, and believe me when I say this: I let you go because that's what you needed. You needed your own space to breathe, to heal. All wounds need air to heal. I was just there to make sure you got it. That's why I let you go. I did it for you, not me. It hurt me and it still does. Everything hurts. Watching you leave and even now, watching you here, hurts."

I felt a weight lifted off my body. It was as if my soul fell out of my body as he spoke. It was a terrible reason, but a valid reason. I did need my own space, but still, my healing process would have been different, perhaps even easier to go through, if I hadn't been alone. My God, how contradicting was I? I left because I couldn't handle being in Miami anymore, let alone around Owen, and next thing I knew, I wanted him to be with me?

I wanted him to save me from myself and soften up the cruel passing of Harper. Maybe I was being too harsh. Maybe I wasn't considering what he was feeling, I thought. But that was the old me thinking, the one who would put herself last and put everyone and their mothers before her. I wasn't like that anymore. I was different, colder, and harder. I wasn't the same drowning flower in the middle of a pond. I had changed, and I wasn't sure it was for the best. All I knew was that I was different, whether I myself accepted it or not.

"You're right. We don't need to do this here or like this. We shouldn't argue," I said. I calmed myself down and took several breaths in and out. He frowned and took a few steps closer but kept his distance. I walked past him, toward Harper's grave, and placed the bouquet of flowers near her tombstone. I felt as if we were disrespecting her, as if the two of us arguing while she was alive wasn't enough.

"I'm sorry for this," I whispered to her as if she were witnessing the collapse of two worlds, the melting of two monuments.

"So what now, Wes? You want me to tell you I'm sorry? That I can't live without you? That I need you? Because I do. I need you," he said.

I couldn't blame him. I was being stubborn, inhumane, and emotionless, but still, a part of me wished all of this had never happened. A part of me still believed in our dreams and hopes and all the plans that we had envisioned for ourselves a few years ago. I was too delicate right now. I was too overwhelmed with everything.

"Oh, Owen," I whimpered as if despair and fear were entering my body at once, despair over my past and fear of my future.

Owen chuckled again as I turned toward him slightly. "I have this memory with Harper," Owen said. I guess he was trying to lift the mood. "And I always find myself coming back to it. It's stupid but I remember it." He smiled and looked at her grave. "Do you remember that one night we were all in New York City and we talked her into skating for the first time?"

"Yes, I remember."

"That night, we had a moment together, and I can't exactly remember it perfectly, but I remember she told me to take care of you. She just had this face, this unforgettable stare, as if she knew, as if she knew she was going to go away. I always think about that moment. I always find myself reminiscing about the way she looked at me. It's almost eerie now when I think about it."

"I really miss her, Owen."

"Yeah, so do I," he said as I looked out through the cemetery.

"Do you think she thought of us when she died? Do you think she was afraid?"

"I don't think so," he said. "She wasn't in the right state of mind at the time, you know?"

"Sometimes I wish she would have told me."

"Yeah," he replied.

"Sometimes I wish it were me instead of her."

"Don't say that, Wes."

"Sometimes, you know, just sometimes I wish she was still here."

The air got clearer the more we spoke, and we talked until I had to go. We both sat by her grave and went on and on about our past. We revisited everything, every month, every year we had gone through together. In a lot of ways, sitting next to Owen reminded me how much I missed him, being with him, with her.

It made me feel whole; it made me feel as if I were young again. Three kids riding their bikes all over Four Quarters, looking for clues to find themselves. It was beautiful, it really was. This moment, for everything it was, was perhaps what I needed. I needed for us to find each other, to collide, to crash and feel something, even if it was a small taste of our past, of what we had and what we still believed in.

"I have to go now," I said. "My flight back home, you know?"

"Yeah, I have to go too. I was only here for a day," he replied as he helped me pick up my belongings.

"Yes, of course." I smiled. Soon afterward, we walked through the park toward the exit. It was such a pretty day outside, different from yesterday and the morning. I went to the ATM inside of the gift shop and cashed out money for my ride to the airport. There was a parked cab already waiting for me on the side of the street. I had made sure there was one right before I left to overcome any delays. Owen helped me with my things and placed everything in the trunk as I got ready to go.

"Well, I guess this is good-bye for now, right?" he said.

"Yes, for now," I said as I looked into his eyes and then gave him a hug.

"It was nice seeing you again, Wes," he murmured into my ear as we held each other on the sidewalk in front of Woodlawn Memorial Park.

"Same," I replied. I held on to him as if I didn't want to let go, as if I wanted to spend a lifetime in this moment forever and ever, till the sun lost its glimmer and the sky became one with the universe.

"Well, okay," I said as our bodies suddenly detached themselves and I found myself opening the cab door. And right before I entered the cab, he said my name. He said my name with such anguish. He said my name as if he knew he was never going to say it ever again.

"Wes." I looked back as if I, too, knew this was the last moment I'd ever hear him call out my name. "I love you. I'll always love you. I hope you know that," he said tenderly. I nodded without saying a single word.

In a lot of ways, our good-bye felt similar to the one we had shared two years earlier. It was unexpected and dry and difficult. It was always hard saying good-bye, because once you said it, you never knew if you would have another opportunity to see that person again. It was also hard for me, at the moment, to tell him I loved him too. I guess a part of me was still hiding behind the walls of solitude I had built. Of course, I felt awful about not saying it back, but that's how it was. That's how it happened—just like that, in an instant. I froze the moment he told me he loved me.

As he stepped back, I entered the cab, and for reasons unknown, all I did was look behind me as he stayed there watching me leave as he had done once before, watching the flame we once had thin itself out into the wind. It hurt, watching him slowly blend into the city as I rode off. It hurt, thinking about how I didn't know when I was going to see him again. It hurt, watching his face one last time as he waved from afar and I waved back.

Good-byes are never easy, and they come so often. Every time I had to let go of someone, it was as if I was abandoning a piece of myself. Every time someone left, one way or another, I, too, stayed behind. It killed me leaving him for a second time, but I still carried hope with me and knew that somewhere down the line, if I believed enough, he and I would be reunited.

It's funny how things end, how life works, and how two people find one another without making any effort at all. And for what it's worth, there are always two sides to the story, two sides of a person and two outcomes to choose from. You can either take what you have and live with it, make the best of it, or you can take what you have and decide that you deserve even more. You can choose to be happy or choose to be sad. You can do what's right for you or what you think is right for you, only to find out it was a bad decision. You can either do this or do that, but in the end, you have to do something.

You have to make a decision, whether the truth is in front of you or not. You have to make your move. You have to take the possibility in all aspects and hope that it will lead you to your perfect laughter, because in the end, you have that kind of power, and you only have one life to make sure it counts.

16

Sometimes words can't express what I feel. Sometimes I feel nothing, and other times I have so much inside me—too much to define. Sometimes I know myself, and other times I don't know who I am and can't recognize the person in the mirror.

Sometimes I find myself in people, places, music, and films. Other times I'm empty and have no connection to the outside world. Sometimes I find myself looking at old photographs, the ones where the three of us are together, smiling without a worry in our hearts.

Those are times I feel something. Those are times I feel this soft little thump beating within my chest, beating for the goodness we're promised, for more. If there is a shot at happiness, then that little beat is why I know it can still be found. I know that, soon enough, I am bound to find my smile once again.

I never saw him again. I never heard from him or heard about him. No matter how much I hoped for it, he never returned to me. He never found me, and I never found him. This bitter earth, I tell you, it's sad how sometimes you have to lose someone and how sometimes things like this aren't avoidable. And when you get down to it, it's all about the way things die, the way they end. Sometimes you want things to work out, but they don't. Sometimes you want things such as moments to keep going and extend themselves for another lifetime, but they don't.

About five years passed and I thought about him less and less, but I never forgot him. I never forgot his messy hair, the way he smiled, and the way he looked into my eyes. I never forgot our childhood and how we both fell in love beneath the starry sky. I never forgot those bright days in the middle of summer riding our bikes together in search of adventure. I never forgot our time together before that one day we accidentally crossed paths on Harper's grave. I never forgot the first time I laid eyes on him and the last time as well. I never forgot the last time he told me he loved me and the last time I told him *in return*. I never forgot him.

I guess you could say I never got over it, but I learned to deal with it as time went on. What we had was special, all of it, from the beginning to the very end, and I never took any of it for granted. I never forgot what we had, and although we were young, dumb and naïve, lost, and confused, I always knew that what we had was real. I always knew that we had meant more. And no, it didn't last forever, but it lasted long enough, and because of it, I appreciated everything, even the bad things.

It was true: I even missed the things he would do to hurt me. The little things that would set me back. The little things he would do like take me for granted and make me feel as if I didn't exist. I missed all of it, everything. I appreciated everything we experienced together in the best way I could.

I eventually made peace with myself and forgave myself for all the things I thought I should have done. That's the thing about growing up. As you grow, you regret your mistakes, but somewhere down the line, you eventually give in. I guess what I'm trying to say is that you learn to value people for what they are, who they are, and what they stand for. You learn how to move on, and most important, you learn how to find salvation in all the things you once believed to be your doom.

In a lot of ways, you learn how even your worst days are important. How they all have some kind of special role in the unfolding of things. How they're all strung together and paint this perfectly imperfect picture, and as you glance at it, you realize how it makes you feel something. How it gives you breath and comforts you when you need it most.

That's how it was when I made peace with them. That's how it was when I finally learned how to let go. It was as if I were being crucified, as if I had set myself up for death and the only person who helped me escape the brutal darkness was myself. One could only assume it wasn't an easy rescue or process. In fact, the transition was a slow, painful one. But as everyone says, "Only time can heal and only time will tell you how it sorts itself out." It did sort itself out. And the more I thought about it, the more I wondered how differently my life would have turned out. Nonetheless, I was grateful for the two of them. I was hopeful of the future and what it had to bring.

I kept visiting Harper's grave. I continued to go at least two times a year, and every time I arrived, I hoped Owen would appear out of nowhere as he had that one time we had crossed paths many moons ago. Of course, he never did, not once.

Many times I thought I saw him, but my mind was playing tricks on me. I guess a part of me wanted to find him, and another part of me kept telling me to move on and let him go, which in the end, I did. I had to.

It wasn't till the last year or so that I finally understood why I left him to begin with, why I moved away from Miami. I understood that it was never because of Harper's death or finding a new beginning in a tragic story. It wasn't because my heart was filled with wanderlust or because I was determined to find some hidden mystical answer to explain where it all went wrong.

No, it wasn't because of them. I had to go because it was the only thing to do, the only thing that made perfect sense, despite what I had gone through and what I believed. I left because of me. I had done it for myself. Leaving was a blessing. It saved me from myself, and because of it, I had a lot to be thankful for. I mean, the whole time I was drowning, I refused to see all the people who were genuinely there for me. The whole time I thought I was alone, and leaving made me appreciate people of all natures, people I considered family and called my friends.

I also learned to appreciate my life for what it was, for the coming and going of people and lovers and friends and opportunities and possibilities. I saw it all as a mystery, and I accepted almost every obstacle that came my way.

At times while visiting Harper, I thought about her father. I thought about the pain he had gone through and how awful it might have been, knowing he probably could have done more. I knew what that was like. I understood that kind of hurting, that kind of regret. I understood how sometimes, you can't control the outcomes for other people. If someone is meant to go, they will go, and there's nothing anyone can do to interfere. I understood how hard it must be for a father to lose his daughter, for a person to lose their best friend and almost lose their very own life over the harsh realities that accompany death. I always wondered about him. I wondered if he continued to write Harper letters, because I never saw them scattered there as I had before. I wondered if he continued to think of her as much as I did. I guess what I'm trying to say is that despite everything I knew or didn't know about him, I ultimately wondered if he was all right.

I kept looking out the window as the plane descended. It was New Year's Eve, and we were just about to land in my hometown of Miami. I was with my father. We had decided to fly down to Miami to spend New Year's Eve with my mother. It was a last-minute decision. I didn't really have a plan, and my father was coming down either way to see my mother.

They had kept a very close relationship after all this time. It was really inspiring and hopeful the way they didn't let a divorce break them apart. I always wanted a bond like that, a bond where friendship was the backbone and no matter what obstacles life threw, you knew you would both survive them no matter how bad things got. To me, that was the ultimate dream, the ultimate way to go through life.

That being said, I was now on the edge of being thirty years old and had been living in New York City for the past three years. Somewhere down the line, my father finally convinced me to come when I lost my teaching job a few years ago. That was a hard year for me, and because of it, I had a lot of choices to make. Thus came the opportunity to make my move to New York City.

At first, it wasn't what I was expecting, but it was a start at a new life. I lived with my father for the first six months, and then I finally saved up enough money to move out on my own. I had a decent job as a professor's assistant at Queensborough Community College for the Physical Therapy program. It wasn't a bad gig, but it wasn't my ideal job.

I worked nights, and sometimes I had to take my work home. Although it wasn't the greatest position, I was blessed to work. Most people I knew were still struggling to find proper employment. I was lucky, so overall I couldn't complain, and there were some perks here and there. I mean, New York wasn't all mediocrity.

I had my father, and no matter how busy we were with our lives, we made time for one another. He was a good support system for me, a real healer, and seeing him at least once a week kept me from wanting to pull my hair out of my skull. We did a lot in the city. We dined. We watched films and even shared a few laughs here and there. Together, my father and I did everything I was supposed to do with Harper and Owen. I owed my life to my father, and during the first year in New York City, he really saved me.

I rooted my feet slowly, and because of it I felt as if I was becoming my old self again.

"Ladies and gentlemen, this is your captain speaking. It's been a pleasure flying with you. I want to wish everyone Happy New Year. Welcome to Miami. Enjoy your stay."

The plane had finally touched ground. Although I was with my father, I was still unfit to fly, and that was probably a part of me I couldn't grow out of. I hated flying, always have and always will. As usual, I'd been paranoid during the entire flight. My father kept talking to me about my mother. He went on about how he was excited to visit her and tell her about his trip to Toronto last summer.

He had brought an entire shoe box filled with pictures he had developed the week before. He was ecstatic about it. He kept repeating the same words over and over, and they kept finding themselves in my ears. He also had a few souvenirs for her. One of them was a giant boot with the Canadian flag painted across it. I thought it was overly exaggerated, not to mention ridiculous.

"I can't wait to show your mom these vacation photos," he said. "I want to make her feel as if she was there, you know?" He must have said that more than fifteen times during the flight. "She's really going to enjoy them."

I couldn't understand his enthusiasm at the time, but I guess all he wanted to do was share a special moment with her. To this day I've never really understood their divorce. I mean, when they were together, they were great, and when they were apart, all my father did was talk about my mother and vice versa. It was strange, but I think it had to happen. I think their separation made them both appreciate one another for who they were. It also brought them even closer, which of course was something that rarely happens. Usually when someone splits, that's it, or they grow to hate one another. That's how it is.

"Looks like it's going to take a few minutes to get off this plane," my father said as he looked behind him and then in front of him as if he were looking for a way out. The funny thing was, everyone in the plane was doing the same thing— like a bunch of birds, one following the other, waiting to see who would fly out first.

A redheaded stewardess wearing a red-and-blue scarf was directing the passengers in first class off the plane. I watched her from my seat on the aisle. I wanted to get off the plane. My legs were tired, and I needed a good cup of coffee. Besides that, the cabin smelled like mildew—like dirty laundry and pesticides. The scent was so strong, it pierced through my nostrils and gave me nausea.

"It shouldn't take that long. I see passengers in the cabin in front exiting already," I said to my father as I peeked over the passenger in front of me. My father did the same and squinted.

"Yeah, you're right. We should be next in no time." His fingers waved through his brittle hair and snapped in front of me as if I hadn't said what I'd just said. It was as if he were trying to grab my attention.

It took about two hours from the plane to the cab to my mother's door. The cab ride was even worse than the flight. I swear, we got every red light in the city, and I got off with whiplash. The tab was almost thirty dollars, which I took care of. We were going to be here for a few days. I didn't have to get back to work till January 4, and my father had enough vacation days to take an entire month off if he wanted to.

My mother jumped through the roof when she first laid eyes on us. She, too, was ecstatic. I could see it in her eyes. She was happy. She was at peace, and having the two of us with her really brightened her up. Her eyes were lit like fireworks sparkling in the dark. It was good seeing her, and after all this time, after everything I had been through, every year I saw her I fell more in love with her smile and the way she shared it with everyone around.

You know, being home made me feel different. By that I mean I could be anywhere in the world, but home gave me this unique feeling, this genuine warmth I never found anywhere else. It also gave me this sense of fiction, as if it wasn't true—a dream, even. I couldn't explain it, but being here with both of my parents made me feel like a small child again, in a good way.

It took me back to when it was just us, before I was exposed to the horrors life brought, before I dipped my feet into pain. Being home made me feel human. It brought me to a place where my vulnerability, brokenness, and sometimes bitterness were a good thing.

As the night continued, we stayed in the living room laughing, drinking, and listening to old Christmas carols. My mother and I were stuffed, and my father had a little too much wine. He was satisfied, and watching him made me smile even more. He, too, had something in his eyes, like a twinkle, a glow, an unbreakable spirit. I couldn't have asked for better company. I was here, in the now, and for once, I wasn't thinking of my past or my future. I wasn't thinking of work or the nice man I had been dating for the past few weeks. In fact, I wasn't thinking about anything at all. I was just feeling, and for the first time in a long time, everything was inspiring.

I was having too much fun. My cheeks were hurting and my abdominal muscles were tight from all the laughter. I wanted to stay in this moment forever, but my eyes were closing and my head was getting heavy. It was almost 3:00 a.m. and I was ready to go to bed. My father had passed out thirty minutes ago on the couch, and my mother was taking care of the dishes. I wanted to help, but she insisted on doing them herself. She wanted me to get some rest, considering I had been on a flight a few hours earlier.

"I had a good time tonight," I said as I walked toward her to give her a good-night hug.

"So did I. It's always nice to have you and your father around," she said. "You two should come here more often."

"I know. It just gets hard with work and all."

"How's that going for you?" She continued to scrub the dishes as the water rushed into the sink.

"It's going well. We just started a new program for disabled patients. We provide intense therapy to improve their quality of life and the students love it," I said.

"Well, that's a good thing. It's always nice to help those in need."

"It doesn't pay much, but it's really rewarding. That's why I do it, you know? To make a difference."

My mother sighed. "I'm really proud of you," she said as she sank her hands into the sink. I nodded and smiled. I got this euphoric feeling knowing how much my mother had acknowledged me. It gave me butterflies.

"Well, I'm going to bed. I'm exhausted."

"Okay, sweetie. Love you." My mother stopped and carefully hugged me without her soapy hands touching me.

"Love you too," I replied. I slowly detached myself from her and walked into my room.

I turned the lights on and quietly closed the door. I scanned my entire room from left to right. Almost everything was how I had left it. I thought it was extremely creepy, not in a bad way, but in a taken-aback kind of way. I thought my mother would have turned my room into an office by now.

On my dresser was a mirror, and on it were several photographs of moments I had shared with both Harper and Owen as children. I walked toward the dresser and picked one specific image of the three of us together. I stood there for a minute analyzing the photo down to the last detail. I remembered the night the photograph was taken. That night was cold. It was one of the first times we visited New York City. We all had mittens on, and Owen's hair was down to his shoulders. I chuckled as I held the photo. Then I turned it around and noticed a faded message written on the back:

We were here. We were together. We were happy. We were alive. Remember this moment.

Remember one another. Remember friendship, and remember love. Fall of 1999.

It was written in Harper's handwriting, and because of that I almost began to cry. It's strange how even the smallest things trigger memories and make you feel like you're suddenly drowning again. It's strange how sometimes you forget to remember once again. How late December can take you to another month of the year. It was sad enough that when she wrote this, she was happy, and knowing that stung a little. I swear, every time I thought about her, it still broke my heart. It never got old and it never broke my heart completely, but it was just enough.

I swear, every time I remembered her, it was as if I had received the news just yesterday. I heard a sudden knock at the door. I wiped my eyes and placed the photograph back on the dresser.

The door cracked. It was my mother. She entered the room quietly. "Hey, you, are you still up?" she said.

"Yeah, I'm here." I wiped my eyes a second time. "I was just—"

"It's okay, dear," she said as she glanced at the photograph I had just misplaced on my dresser.

"Yeah," I said, stumbling over the word a little.

"There's something I wanted to give you," she whispered as she reached toward the back of her bathrobe and revealed a sealed envelope with a little heart on it. I recognized it from a mile away.

"Is this—" I said, dazed and confused.

"Yes, yes it is."

"But how?"

"A few months ago her mother came here distorted and confused. Poor woman, she's a bit delusional now. Anyway, she came here knocking and I felt terrible for her, for everything. So I opened the door and let her in. We shared a glass of wine and began to talk. She opened up about a lot of things, perhaps even things she couldn't believe she had done. Poor thing, she kept blaming herself for Harper." I kind of knew where that was coming from, in some shape or form; everyone kind of blamed themselves for Harper.

"She said the night she found her daughter's body in her room, Harper had this note in her hand. Apparently it was for you. It still has your name on the back of it, see?" My mother flipped the envelope over and continued. "She said she held on to it to protect Harper, which is why you're just receiving it now. You know, dear, it breaks my heart thinking about her. She was full of life. And I'm sorry. I can only imagine what you're feeling right now, especially since I'm giving you this letter now, during the holidays, but I felt that instead of mailing it to you, I would rather give it to you in person."

Seeing the envelope hit me hard. It felt like a massive tidal wave swallowing the entire beach and I was nothing more than a small girl caught in the middle of the shore. It devoured me, suddenly, at once, and without regret. This untamable force was indescribable. I felt as if I had been knocked into another realm of reality, one where physics and logic didn't exist. Even after all the drama I've been through, I wasn't sure if this was acceptable.

"Mom," I said, swallowing whatever sense of myself I had left.

"I'm sorry I'm giving this to you now," she repeated as she extended her hand. I was in shock. A part of me didn't want to take that letter. A part of me didn't want to take that risk again, to open Pandora's box and fall back into where I had been a few years ago.

"It's okay, baby, take it. It's for you." I reached out and opened my hand, hesitating as I wondered if this was a good idea.

My mother sighed. "You know, she really loved you, Wes, and you really loved her. And some of my best memories are of watching the two of you play. What you two had was special. It's such a shame that she did that to herself, that she cut her own life short." My mother frowned.

I didn't have a response. I was too much in shock to say anything as my arm slowly reeled itself back in.

"It would be a shame if you don't give her the honor of this. I'm sure it's something you need to read," she said as she placed the envelope on my bed. "Well, I have to get some rest now. Good night, honey. I love you." She leaned over me, and her lips pressed against my right cheek. In an instant she was gone, and I suddenly came to my senses. My mother was right. Whatever Harper had written for me was probably something I needed to read, something to give me closure. I got up from my bed. I locked the door and looked back toward the letter. Overwhelmed, I grabbed it and held on to it.

"Harper, I wish I could have saved you," I whispered as I took a deep breath, ripped open the letter, and never looked back.

My dearest friend,

I can only hope this letter reaches you in a timely manner, and for the record, I don't know how to start this. Like Owen, I've never been any good at this, but hey, let me give it a try.

Where to start? How about back to the beginning? Okay, well, for the past few years I've been slowly deteriorating. I have this problem, this disease. Now, I know it's going to be hard for you to take in, considering I never told you, or anyone, for that matter. For that I'm deeply sorry. Believe me when I tell you that keeping this from you was one of the hardest things. This year, it's been really aggressive. I've had a lot of trouble doing things I usually do—you know, normal things, like eating and walking, etc., and it's really hard for me to pretend like everything is okay. This is why I've been so distant lately.

There's no cure for what I have, and there's no information, really, which doesn't give my future much hope. I feel like my life will become dust. I feel like the faint glow of a dying candle. What good am I? I'm really depressed, Wes, and I'm hurting and I refuse to take you with me toward the dark, horrid, painful tunnel I'm meant for. I'm sorry for this, Wes. I hope you find it in yourself to forgive me. I hope you learn to let this go. I hope you find what you love, and I hope you live your life without regret. I hope you don't confuse love with lust, and I hope whatever happens, you find the courage to smile again.

I'm sorry for everything. If there was anyone who could have stopped me or saved me, that person would have been you. I hope one day, we find each other again and laugh over whatever pain we might have caused.

I love you, until we meet again.
Harper

I don't know much about this world. I don't know why we feel the things we feel or why we feel things the way we do. I don't know why we behave a certain way and why certain people bring certain things out of us. I don't know why some people change or why some people wake up to do the same things over and over. I don't know why we laugh or why we cry or why we smile or why we hurt. I don't know what makes people care about other people, and I don't know why those same people never find it in themselves to stay.

I don't know why life sometimes seems unfulfilling, and I don't know why most of the time I don't have enough words in me to describe how these things go. They say a picture is worth a thousand words, and I can't seem to wonder how sometimes I see a thousand different things and yet none of them define the things I feel.

Like I said, I don't know what makes the world go around and maybe no one ever will, but I do know one thing. I know some people give you the hope and the courage you need to express what you have within. I know some people define you, that is, your thoughts and your actions. I know some people are made of more than just flesh and bone. I know some people make you realize that nothing really matters but the ways they make you feel and that some people need other people to feel at home. And I believe that's what counts. That's what's important here. You live your life lost and confused, but in the end, you live your life with certain people who complete you, who guide you, who bring out the best version of you even if you don't know it for yourself.

And no matter how much you close yourself in, there will always be some people who make you feel as if you're not alone, as if you have someone with you, because ultimately, you do. And it's beautiful how you go through the fire with these certain people no matter how much it burns. You rely on their trust and they rely on yours, and to be honest, there's nothing more satisfying than that. That alone makes this lonely life worth living, and that's all I have to say about that.

17

Sometimes the love of your life isn't really the love of your life. Sometimes you think you belong to someone only to discover that somewhere down the line you don't, that that person is there only to prepare you for someone greater, for someone different and someone you were born for. Sometimes you think it's the end of the world only to find out that it is really the beginning. Sometimes old things teach you new things, and sometimes new things mean nothing at all.

Sometimes the past gives you the strength to face the future, and sometimes the future is brighter than you think it is. Sometimes when you think you know something, it only means you know nothing at all, and sometimes you arrive only to find out you never even left to begin with. Sometimes what you love isn't good for you, and sometimes what's bad heals you in ways you never would have imagined.

Sometimes when you fall, you fly, and sometimes when you break, you do because you're slowly gathering yourself back together again. Sometimes mistakes don't teach you much, and sometimes the smallest of things hold revelations that are too hard to ignore. Sometimes there's so much in you that you don't know where to begin, and sometimes when you finally begin, it feels as if it is already too late to get going. Sometimes you love the wrong people, and other times the wrong people bring you peace. And last but not least, sometimes you have to let go and free yourself in order to begin all over again.

I moved to San Francisco nine years ago. It was another one of those things, a blind opportunity. Again, I had lost my job back in New York City, and the stars were aligned, and something inside of me was telling me to move out west. At first, it was hard to get it together. Finding a job again was nearly impossible, as was making friends, and among other things, getting used to the time zone took some time, but of course I learned to hold it together.

I was living off my savings in a one-bedroom apartment near Chinatown. It wasn't what I'd originally wanted, but it was a roof over my head, and it allowed me time to figure out my next move. I was definitely patiently living day by day in the great golden city. I was doing new things, finding new places, discovering parts of myself I never knew existed. I was pretty much learning how to live again. I went through this self-transformation every time I moved to a new city. I would morph into a completely different person, a better person.

The first year was definitely the hardest and most unpredictable. A lot of things happened that year and a lot of things changed, and it all happened fast, so fast that I had no idea where I was going until I was consumed and it was too late.

During my second year of living in San Francisco, I met a man named Christopher White. He was a South American man born and raised in Seattle. He was about two years older than me and so tall that he hovered over me. His hair was dark and slightly trimmed, and he always smelled like control and masculinity. He was educated, full of drive and ambition. He was caring and genuinely wanted what was best for other people. That was one of the things that drove me toward him: the way he would take his time to delicately aid someone in need. Whether it was a talk or going out of his way to do a favor, he was for the people. I loved that about him. I also loved how no matter where he was, he was always alert to his surroundings.

He also had a lot of good energy and spark to get my fire going. At times, he was intense but for good reasons. He was a lover and a listener and was always there for me when I needed him most. One could say he was everything I was looking for or, rather, everything I didn't know I needed until the first time we met.

I met him one day while visiting Harper. It was almost as if fate had decided when and where we were going to meet. Now, looking back, I believe the timing was too perfect.

I was on my way out of Woodlawn Memorial Park when suddenly he appeared in the middle of the rain. I was running toward the trolley when I accidentally stepped over a puddle. Of course, it had to be a small pothole; of course, I had to slip and almost land on the ground, but thankfully I didn't. Within seconds I had shaken myself off, and that's when he came to my aid. I guess he had been watching me from afar and I guess one could say we had been drawn to one another ever since. Soon enough, he swept me off my feet, and even sooner, I feel in love with him, all of him.

The process was simple. There were no games, there was no confusion, nothing could disengage our fire. It was easy, we were easy, and everything just fell into place. He erased and rewrote everything for me. From the way I saw the world to the way I had to let go of it, Christopher arrived to me like a comet, lighting my sky, soaring through it as if the wish of all wishes had come true. In a lot of ways, he saved me. He gave me hope when I needed it most. He gave me vision and taught me about self-love and self-forgiveness.

Yes, at my age, I still had a lot of learning to do, a lot of discovering and self-healing to explore. In other words, I loved him dearly, and I loved myself even more.

We spent countless days and nights where he would visit me and I would visit him. We always made sure we had *our* time together. We made sure nothing was taken for granted, and we always made sure we were open with each other. After all, our well-being and happiness always came first, and thankfully we were both old enough to understand that. Because of that, we had a strong bond, and I couldn't even imagine what my life would become without it. It was perfect. It was beautiful. Yes, there were times when we weren't on the same page. There were times when one of us would wander off because we had let our worst out, but hey, that's life, right? That's love, right?

Nonetheless, we would always come back to one another and make it work. That's how I knew it was real. We never went too far off. We went only as far as our eyes could see.

We dated for a few years and eventually, he asked me to marry him. Soon afterward, we had a daughter named Sevyn. She's five years old now, and like most children she's full of curiosity and carries an imagination full of depth. She's exactly like me, identical, so much that it almost scares me. Like me, she wants to control everything, she wants to understand without knowing how much time it takes to analyze and break things down. Like me, she wants everything now, now, now.

And what's funny about her is that at times, she wants everything but doesn't understand what to do with it. She wants answers but doesn't ask the right questions. She wants a star in the palm of her hand, but she doesn't fly long enough to claim one as her own. She was the same way when she was a baby. She wanted to walk without knowing how to crawl, she wanted to run before knowing how to walk, and so on and so forth. Children, like most parents, take more than they can handle, and because of it, they fall the same way adults fall, to learn.

The three of us did everything together. From dawn to dusk we were inseparable, the same way Owen, Harper, and I were when we were children. Sevyn brought out my inner child, Christopher made me feel free, and together we were happy. I was happy, genuinely happy, and my life couldn't have been any better. Of course, every once in a while I found myself thinking of them, and of course, when I was alone, awake in the middle of the night, I thought about my old life.

I thought about the inconsistencies and how my old life gave me a run for my money. I thought about Harper and where she would be and where I would be if we had done what we had set out to do. I thought about that one night, while we were together at Rockefeller Center beneath the stars. I thought about our lazy summer days, the ones we spent passing through our adolescence and trying to figure out where the scars came from, the ones marked beneath our battered chests. I thought about the way they made me feel, the way a smile changed a life, and the way the connection between two people grew. I thought about love and how sometimes even the slightest glance of it could destroy the world but also save it.

I thought about Harper in the most random of ways as well. There was always something that reminded me of her, and those coincidences never stopped reaching me, because the more I went on to live my life, the older I grew, the more I felt as if Harper was looking after me, protecting me from harm from the other side. Something would always remind me of her, and it would always push me back where I belonged.

What defeated me in many ways was when I learned about Owen's death about a year ago. A mutual friend informed me that Owen had been battling cancer for the past several years. I didn't know about it. When I found out about his death last summer, it devastated me, and knowing I hadn't been there for him was even worse.

For months, I couldn't believe it, and the guilt consumed my heart beyond control. I felt guilty for many reasons: one, for leaving him behind; two, for never trying to reach out, no matter how much I wanted to; and three, for blocking him out completely. But the biggest reason I felt guilty was because of how I'd acted on that last day I saw him while leaving Woodlawn a few years back. Right before I entered the cab, he told me how much he loved me. I felt the same way at the time, but for some strange reason, one I do not understand to this day, I said nothing. I froze, gave him a cold shoulder, and left, just like that.

I vanished into my own life. It hurts that that was the last moment we spent together. And it kills me that I never told him how much I loved him, how much I missed him, and how much he meant to me. It kills me that he never knew how many sleepless nights I lived through because the thought of him kept me up all night.

It kills me, because after all this time, I had a lot to say to him and never got around to doing so. It kills me because, for me, the end of my world happens at least once every two weeks since he's been gone. It kills me because I really meant all the things I told him when we were children. It kills me because sometimes I feel that without him here, somewhere in the vastness of it all, there is no me. It kills me because it hurts, but I'm still breathing.

It kills me because they say "letting go" will "help me," but all I can do is think about him. And last but not least, his death kills me because sometimes, deep down inside, I feel like I still love him, but he is not here.

The regret of not being there for him had ahold of me for many months. I felt horrible, because no matter how much time passed, no matter how hard I loved my husband, no matter how many people I lost or met, I had done what I shouldn't have. I had gotten so caught up with my own life that I forgot what and who was important. Sometimes, if you're not careful about the people you love, you tend to ignore them and take them for granted. And like I said, it doesn't matter what you've been through, where you came from, or where you're going. Sometimes, you don't know what you have until it's gone, and most of the time you're never quite ready for its sudden good-bye.

My daughter and I visited Harper's grave every other week. We went on Saturdays during the afternoon; it became a ritual for us. We would wake up early and go to the zoo or the beach, and in between we would get some lunch, and then we would finish our day with visiting Harper's grave. Of course, I didn't expect a five-year-old child to understand death or loss, but I always told her we had to visit her auntie.

Every other Saturday we would go, and every other Saturday Sevyn believed it was an adventure. It's beautiful the way a child sees the world, the way their innocence overpowers even the harshest realities. It's beautiful how they smile when they see you cry, when they see you break when you believe no one is around. It's beautiful how they bring out the sun and sometimes make you forget where you are. Sometimes little Sevyn made everything go away, and the more we went together, the more I realized that sometimes a child's eyes have more answers than anyone else you've ever known.

Today was like any other day here in the gloomy city of San Francisco. It was slightly chilly, and the salt from the Pacific air filled our lungs. Today, we woke up a little earlier than usual.

Today, we walked across the Golden Gate Bridge four times, and after that we went to the Exploratorium, and soon after that we took a public trolley to Fisherman's Wharf, where we had lunch. We ate clam chowder and watched the seals for hours to end our day in Woodlawn Memorial Park. It was there where I always found tranquility and she always found something to make me smile.

"Why do we always have to come here, Mama?" Sevyn said in a thin, high-pitched voice. From time to time she would ask this very same question, and I would always reply with the same answer. The thing about being a mother is, you have to unlearn everything you've ever known. You have to see life through the eyes of a child. You have to ask the same questions they do and gather enough words to execute the perfect answer. And the funny thing is, I'm still learning. I'm still a student, and I still don't know what to make of it entirely, that is, this life and what it is meant for.

"We come here because I made a promise to your auntie Harper," I replied, holding Sevyn's left hand as we walked toward Harper's grave site. "Do you remember what we do every time we come here?"

"Yes! We read her a bedtime story," Sevyn said as her hair brushed against her face.

I laughed at her response. "No, we don't read her a bedtime story. We come to keep her a little company," I explained as we suddenly stood still and I fixed her hair.

"Only for a little while, right, Mama?"

"Yes, for a little while."

"Mama, sometimes when we are home with Daddy, I miss Auntie Harper," Sevyn said as she plucked and collected little yellow flowers.

"Me too, baby, me too," I said, placing my hand on her shoulder as we continued to walk to my best friend's final resting place.

As the years continued to stack themselves atop one another, I wished for a lot of things. I wished for infinite happiness, infinite laughter, and infinite love. But of all the things I wished for, nothing ever amounted to the kind of wishful dreaming I did when I thought of them.

I wished Harper could have been there when I got married, and I wished she could have been there to carry my firstborn. I wished she had been there when I needed her most, and I wish I could have been there for her when she felt alone. I wish I could have watched her enjoy her life, and I wished she could have lived long enough to do what she loved. I wished things could have stayed the same, and I wished none of it had changed.

Owen wasn't far away either, for I also wished he and I had stayed close, and I wished I could have been there during his ill days. I wished he'd been happy during our time apart, and I wished he had found some kind of peace somewhere down the line. And to top things off, I always wished I could have gone back one last time, and I wished the three of us could have stayed children forever. I wished things weren't so hard, and I wished it was easier to find other people to fill that void.

And in the end, I kept wishing. I kept getting older, and I kept watching my daughter grow older. I kept searching for more, kept going, and I kept remembering Harper for who she was. I kept visiting her, and I never forgot my promise. I never forgot her, and I always honored what we had.

And of all the things people told me throughout the years, ironically enough, I also never forgot what the cabdriver told me during that one visit to San Francisco when I ran into Harper's father and Owen. I never forgot the words, the ones he shared with me right before I entered Woodlawn Memorial Park for the second time. I never forgot how he carefully said that all of us, dead or alive, carry this force, this attraction, this gravity, and how this force brings the people who are meant to be in your life together.

Those words stayed with me forever. They were engraved in my bones, and deep down inside I always knew that one day I would be reunited with my friends. I knew that one day, in some thread of time, we would all find each other again, and we would laugh together, and it would be as if we were seeing each other for the very first time.

Sometimes all we have is the past to help us move forward, and sometimes all we can ever do is hope for a better tomorrow.

CPSIA information can be obtained
at www.ICGtesting.com
Printed in the USA
LVOW03s0908180417
531165LV00002B/2/P